Costume Catastrophe

by

Kathi Daley

This book is dedicated to everyone who
loves Halloween as much as I do.

I want to thank the very talented Jessica Fischer for the cover art.

I so appreciate Bruce Curran, who is always ready and willing to answer my cyber questions.

And, of course, thanks to the readers and bloggers in my life, who make doing what I do possible.

Thank you to Randy Ladenheim-Gil for the editing.

Special thanks to Jeanie Daniel, Nancy Farris, Robin Coxon, and Connie Correll for submitting recipes.

And finally I want to thank my sister Christy for always lending an ear and my husband Ken for allowing me time to write by taking care of everything else.

Books by Kathi Daley

Come for the murder, stay
for the romance.

Zoe Donovan Cozy Mystery:

Halloween Hijinks
The Trouble With Turkeys
Christmas Crazy
Cupid's Curse
Big Bunny Bump-off
Beach Blanket Barbie
Maui Madness
Derby Divas
Haunted Hamlet
Turkeys, Tuxes, and Tabbies
Christmas Cozy
Alaskan Alliance
Matrimony Meltdown
Soul Surrender
Heavenly Honeymoon
Hopscotch Homicide
Ghostly Graveyard
Santa Sleuth
Shamrock Shenanigans
Kitten Kaboodle
Costume Catastrophe
Candy Cane Caper – October 2016

Whales and Tails Cozy Mystery:

Romeow and Juliet
The Mad Catter
Grimm's Furry Tail
Much Ado About Felines
Legend of Tabby Hollow
Cat of Christmas Past
A Tale of Two Tabbies
The Great Catsby
Count Catula – *September 2016*
Cat of Christmas Present – *November 2016*

Seacliff High Mystery:

The Secret
The Curse
The Relic
The Conspiracy
The Grudge

Sand and Sea Hawaiian Mystery:

Murder at Dolphin Bay
Murder at Sunrise Beach
Murder at the Witching Hour – *September 2016*

Zimmerman Academy:
The New Normal

Ashton Falls Cozy Cookbook

Road to Christmas Romance:
Road to Christmas Past

From Henery Press:
Pumpkins in Paradise
Snowmen in Paradise
Bikinis in Paradise
Christmas in Paradise
Puppies in Paradise
Halloween in Paradise
Treasure in Paradise – April 2017

Chapter 1

Monday, October 24

"We could still go with the chubby pumpkin costume," I suggested to my best friend, Ellie Davis, as I tried to help her squeeze into a sexy vampire costume that was never going to fit.

"I'm not chubby," Ellie insisted as she stood in front of the full-length mirror in the dressing room of the local costume shop, sucking in her stomach.

"I know, but you *are* three months pregnant. This costume isn't going to fit no matter how much you suck in your stomach."

"If I go as the chubby pumpkin people will know. It's the classic costume for pregnant women."

"No one will know."

"They will."

"Okay, how about a ghost? We'll just grab a sheet, cut out some eye holes, and you'll be good to go."

Ellie started crying.

Again.

I knew it was the pregnancy hormones, but seriously? If I was going to cry at every little thing when I got pregnant I was going to go back on the Pill before it was too late. Of course Ellie wasn't just pregnant; she had a secret—a very big, life-altering secret she'd already kept much too long.

"Don't cry; we'll figure this out." I tried for an encouraging tone. "We'll keep looking until we find the perfect thing."

"It's no use," Ellie sobbed. "I look like a whale. I'll just skip the party and stay home. It's really the only logical choice."

"You're not staying home and you don't look like a whale. In fact, other than the tiny baby bump you don't look any different at all. Still, it's not going to be too long before even the baggiest sweaters fail to hide your secret." I took Ellie's hand and led her over to the little bench that ran along one wall. I sat down, pulling her down beside me. "You know I love you and you know I'll do anything for you, but it seems to me that your current dilemma might serve as a hint that it really is time."

"I can't."

"You can and you should. Levi has a right to know." I referred to the baby's father, my other best friend, Levi Denton.

Ellie took a deep breath. Then she let it out slowly. "I know. I'll tell him. I promise. I just need to find the right time."

"Now seems like as good a time as any."

"No. Not now. He has the big game against Bryton Lake this week. I don't want to distract him. I'll tell him after." Levi was the head coach for the Ashton Falls High School varsity football team.

I gave Ellie's hand a squeeze. "Okay. I guess it can wait another week. But we really do need to find you a costume for the party. You mentioned a whale. You know, a whale actually might be the perfect costume."

Ellie started crying again.

Good going, Zoe.

"How about we take a break? We'll go get something to eat and maybe we can try costume shopping again another day."

"Okay." Ellie dried her eyes with the back of her hand. "I guess I am hungry."

"It's a beautiful fall evening. How about we eat at Rosie's and then take a walk along Main and look at all the decorations? I just love it when the town is lit up for Halloween. The merchants have gone all out with the windows, and I heard the gazebo in the park is lit up with orange and white twinkle lights."

"Okay. Just let me change back into my clothes."

"I want to look for some lights for the front of the house." My husband, Zak Zimmerman, in usual Zak fashion, had gone Halloween crazy, stringing all the lights we had around the pool and patio in the back of the house. "I'll meet you up front."

"Can you grab some lights for the boathouse? I think I'm going to decorate this year. Seems like the baby and I need to start some new traditions."

I smiled. "That sounds like a wonderful idea. I'll even help you put them up."

After I left the dressing room I headed toward the decorations. I know at times I give Zak a hard time for being so Halloween crazy, but the truth is that I find his enthusiasm sweet and charming. Of course we're at the point where we're going to have to build a second garage or at least a shed on the property to store everything, but there's no denying the Zimmerman house is the sincerest at the lake.

"Zoe?" someone said from behind me. "Zoe Donovan?"

I turned around. "Rachael." I hugged the woman I hadn't seen since she'd left the area more than ten years earlier. "How are you?"

"I'm great."

I looked at the young girl clinging to her hand. "Is that your daughter?"

"It is. This is Joslyn."

"I'm so happy to meet you, Joslyn."

"It's nice to meet you too."

I looked at Rachael. "Are you in town for the Haunted Hamlet celebration?"

"Actually, Joslyn and I have moved back to Ashton Falls. My aunt passed away last year and left me her house. At first I planned to sell it, but Jos and I talked it over and decided to give small-town living a try. We only just arrived last week, but so far we're enjoying the decorations and the holiday feel very much."

"Well, I for one am happy you're back. And you picked a great time to arrive. We have a lot of really awesome events planned for the weekend."

"Will there be a pumpkin patch?" Joslyn asked.

"There will. And a hay bale maze and hayrides. If you're the brave sort, there'll be an awesome haunted house as well as a chili cook-off and a bake sale. There really is something for everyone. Is it just the two of you?"

"Yes," Joslyn answered. "I don't have a dad."

I glanced at Rachael.

"He was never in the picture, but Jos and I have done great on our own."

"I'm sure you have." I looked back to the girl, who had bright blue eyes and long brown hair. "So, are you attending Ashton Falls Elementary?"

The girl nodded. "I'm planning to go there beginning next week. I'm in the fifth grade."

If Joslyn was in the fifth grade chances were Rachael had been pregnant with her before she graduated high school. Actually, that would explain a lot. She'd simply disappeared after graduation. I'd figured she'd gone off to college, but her parents had remained in town for a couple more years before moving to Florida and she'd never once come to visit that I knew of.

"I heard you got married last year," Rachael commented. "Any little ones on the way?"

"No. Not yet. Although Zak and I do have two minors living with us." I made eye contact with Joslyn. "Scooter is in the sixth grade. He's an energetic sort. I'm sure you'll meet him. Zak and I also have a twelve-year-old girl named Alex living with us. She attends Zimmerman Academy, but I'd be willing to bet she'd be happy to show you around if you'd like."

"I'd like that."

"I heard you started your own private school," Rachael joined in. "How's that going?"

"Good. The actual construction of the new facility has had a few setbacks, so the dorms aren't open quite yet, but we've managed to recruit a bunch of local families to temporarily board students, so we started offering a full class schedule beginning this semester. I'd love to tell you more about the school and catch up in general. We should make plans to get together soon. I'm sure Zak would like to say hi."

"I'd like to. It'll be nice to catch up with old friends. Is Levi Denton still in town?"

Suddenly I remembered that Rachael and Levi had dated senior year. I looked at Joslyn. She definitely had the same coloring as Levi. Surely he couldn't be... "Yeah, Levi still lives here. He's coaching football over at the high school."

"And Joey?"

Joey Waverly and Levi had been good friends in high school, both starting players on the football team.

"Yup, he's still around too. He married Margo Margolis right out of high school, but they got divorced almost a year ago. Joey works for the electric company."

"And Tommy Payton?"

Tommy also had been on the football team, and, if I remembered correctly, also dated Rachael for a while. "He no longer lives in Ashton Falls, but I heard he's in town right now. Ashton Falls High is playing Bryton Lake on Friday and the winner will take first place and therefore go on to regionals. We really should have a dinner party so everyone can catch up."

Rachael diverted her eyes and then looked down at her watch. "Geez, I gotta go. It was fun running into you. Let's do get together soon. I'm pretty busy getting settled in, but it would be fun to catch up with everyone. I'll text you my number."

I watched as Rachael grabbed her daughter and dashed out the front door of the Halloween store.

"Was that Rachael Conway?" Ellie asked after joining me.

"Yeah. Can you believe Rachael has a fifth grader?"

"Wow, she must have gotten pregnant right out of high school. I didn't even know she was seriously dating anyone."

"She said the dad wasn't in the picture."

"That's too bad. We should invite her to go to lunch with us. Will she be in town long?"

"Actually, she's moved back. She said her aunt left her the house she owned over on Maple."

Ellie frowned. She and I had both hung out with Rachael quite a bit when we were in school, especially during the time when Rachael had been dating Levi. We'd all gotten along really well, although Ellie and Levi hadn't been a couple at that time. Not that Ellie and Levi were dating now, but they were definitely more than just friends. I had to wonder what Ellie *really* thought about Rachael being back in town.

"We should probably get going," I suggested. "Just let me pay for this and then we'll head to Rosie's."

"I think I'm going to grab some of those scarecrows for my front deck, and maybe one of those flower arrangements for the dining table." Ellie traded her frown for a genuine smile. "All of a sudden I'm feeling excited about the upcoming holiday."

"I'm glad. Let's get a wreath for your door while we're at it."

We gathered everything we'd chosen and got into what looked to be an endless line. Every year I think I'm going to get an earlier start on Halloween, and every year life seems to get in the way and I find myself scrambling once again. I tossed a couple of bags of the candy that had been conveniently displayed along the area roped off for the line in my basket. Ellie grabbed a bag of her own, which she opened and proceeded to eat half of before we reached the register. I guess she was eating for two, but I had to question how much food a baby that weighed less than a pound really required. Ellie had a lot of nervous energy and a naturally high metabolism, but if she continued to eat the way she had been the past few weeks she was going to have more than baby weight to worry about.

We paid for our purchases, then drove through town to Rosie's, which was decorated with its own seasonal displays, including a creative bunch of jack-o'-lanterns. We settled into a booth at the front of the restaurant and decided on the advertised special of the day. Once we'd ordered and our food had been delivered our conversation returned to the idea of

Halloween costumes and roomy alternatives.

"I think I'll look through my closet to see if I can come up with a costume using things I already have," Ellie said as she dove into the pile of pasta on her plate. "Or maybe I'll make something. I've been in the mood to sew lately."

"That might be a good idea. You're creative, but it's only a week until Halloween. I just hope I can get everything I need to get done between now and then."

"How's the haunted house coming along?" Ellie asked after biting into a giant meatball.

I grinned. "It's going to be our best one yet. I have to hand it to Levi. He really did find the perfect location. And the best part is, as far as I know, the house we're using isn't haunted and hasn't been associated with any murders, which means we may actually be able to keep it open the entire weekend." The past three haunted houses sponsored by the Ashton Falls Events Committee had been shut down before we'd really gotten going due to very real murders occurring before opening day. "It'll take a bit of effort on our part to have it ready for the weekend, but I think we can do it."

"Just let me know what you need me to do. Are you going to finish your garlic bread?"

I passed the bread to my seemingly starving friend. "Levi said he was going to pick up the keys today, so we should be able to start decorating tomorrow. Jeremy is still on his honeymoon, so I need to be at the Zoo until five, but I plan to head straight to the house after that to start the spookification process. If you want to come along we can ride together."

"I'm free. Just plan to pick me up at the boathouse. Have you talked to Jeremy? Are they having a good time?"

"I haven't talked to him in over a week, but the last time I did speak to him he said they were having a wonderful time." Jeremy Fisher, my assistant at Zoe's Zoo, the wild and domestic animal rescue and rehabilitation shelter I own, had married his longtime girlfriend, Jessica Anderson, two weekends before. Jessica and Jeremy had decided to include a Disney cruise for their honeymoon so that Jessica's daughter, Rosalie, and Jeremy's daughter, Morgan Rose, could go along. The new family was due back the following Thursday.

"I'm not sure I'd want to go on a cruise. The thought of being out at sea for days at a time makes me feel claustrophobic," Ellie commented.

"I know the cruise they chose makes a lot of stops, but I get what you're saying. I wouldn't really want to do a cruise either, although based on the photos Jeremy has sent, it does look like something Alex and Scooter would enjoy very much."

Ellie put her hand on her stomach. "It still seems so odd that it won't be all that long before I'll be taking my son or daughter's enjoyment into account."

"Have you decided whether to find out the baby's sex?"

"My doctor said we could do an ultrasound at around eighteen weeks. I think I want to know. It will make planning easier."

"I'm so excited to be an honorary auntie. We'll have to have a shower when it gets closer. They have such cute things for babies these days."

Ellie smiled. "Don't go too crazy. I'm going to have a serious space issue. I took some measurements and I think I can fit a crib and changing table in the loft next to my bed, but I guess I'll have to move eventually."

It made me sad that my best friend would no longer be just down the beach. My grandfather still technically owned the boathouse. Maybe I'd ask him if it was okay with him if we built an addition onto the tiny structure. The property the boathouse sat on was huge, so land coverage shouldn't be a problem.

I decided not to suggest a remodel until I had a chance to speak to both my grandfather and Zak, so I changed the subject. "I'm going to run to the powder room while you finish up and then we'll pay the check and take a walk like we planned."

"One of the waitresses who worked here when I did is manning the cash register tonight. I want to stop and chat with her for a minute, so I'll take care of the check. I'll meet you up front."

I handed Ellie a couple of twenty-dollar bills. "Okay, but I'm paying for dinner. It's my turn and we agreed. I'll just be a few minutes."

Of course when you live in a small town and your intention is to make your way from the front of a popular restaurant to the back, it can take more than a few minutes because at almost every table you pass are seated friends wanting to waylay you to say hi. It was fifteen minutes later that I finally made my way back to the front of the eatery.

"Did you see where Ellie went?" I asked the young hostess who was standing near the front door.

"She wanted me to tell you that she went down the street to Gilda's." The girl, who looked to still be in high school, was texting the entire time she spoke to me. "She said she needed to ask Gilda about something, so she figured you could just meet her there."

"Okay, thanks." Gilda Reynolds owned Bears and Beavers, a popular touristy type shop that sold everything you could think of having to do with bears and beavers. The shop was only a few doors down from Rosie's.

"Oh, and a woman came in and gave me this to give to you," she added without ever looking up.

I took the folded sheet of notepaper from the girl. I opened it and read the cryptic message: *One has died; others will follow unless you can stop it.*

I frowned. "Who gave this to you?"

The girl shrugged. "Just some lady. I've never seen her before. I'm pretty sure she's from out of town. She had an accent."

"What sort of accent?"

"I don't know. British maybe. I'm not good at figuring out accents."

I looked at the note again. No one with a British accent came to mind. "What did she look like?"

The girl finally looked up from her phone.

"I don't know. I guess she was about thirty-five or forty. She had dark hair about shoulder length and was wearing a blue sweater and a pair of black jeans. I really didn't pay that much attention, but she was just here a couple of minutes ago, so she may still be around."

"What exactly did she say?"

The girl blew her long bangs out of her eyes. Then she looked toward the ceiling, as if trying to remember. "She asked if Zoe Donovan was here. I told her I thought you were in the ladies' room. She said a woman had come up to her, handed her the note, and asked her to give it to you. She said she was in a rush and asked if I could pass it along. I said I would and now I have."

I looked at the note again. It could be a prank, but the chills running up my spine seemed to indicate that it wasn't. *One has died.* I had to wonder who. "Did she say anything else?"

"Nope, that's it."

"Did she mention what the woman who gave her the note looked like?"

"Like I said, she only said to give you the note and then she left."

The phone on the reception desk rang. The girl picked it up. "Rosie's Café."

I pulled on my sweater and headed down the street. It was obvious I wasn't going to get any more information out of the girl. I looked up and down the street as I headed for Bears and Beavers. There were a lot of people out looking at the lights and taking advantage of the beautiful autumn evening, but I didn't see anyone with dark hair and a blue sweater.

"There you are," Ellie greeted me when I entered the store. "I was about to come looking for you."

"Did either of you see a woman with dark hair, dark jeans, and a blue sweater?" I asked the pair.

"Not me," Ellie answered.

"Me either," Gilda seconded. "Why?"

I handed Gilda the note. Ellie read it over her shoulder. Both women looked at me.

"Where did you get this?" Ellie asked.

I explained about the woman in the blue sweater and the totally clueless girl who was working as a hostess at Rosie's.

"This must be a prank," Ellie said.

"Yeah, it has to be," Gilda added. "It's just too odd that someone would leave a note like this for you at Rosie's. I mean, who even knew you would be there?"

"I don't know, but the girl at the hostess station did say the woman who left the note asked for me by name. Maybe someone followed Ellie and me from the costume shop, or maybe a passerby saw us sitting inside and decided to leave the note."

"The whole thing is bizarre," Gilda insisted. "It has to be a prank."

"Maybe. But what if it isn't?"

Ellie looked down at the note again. "If someone wanted you to take action, to do something to prevent these deaths, it seems like they would have provided you with more information. This is so vague. It has to be a prank. Maybe one of the kids at Zimmerman Academy. Everyone knows you seem to get wrapped up in a murder investigation every year at about this time. Maybe one of the kids is just pulling your leg."

I took the note back from Ellie and looked at it again. I remembered the past three Halloweens, when there had been three very real deaths to investigate. I wanted to believe the note was a prank, but deep in my gut I suspected it wasn't. For one thing, my Zodar was on full alert, and if there was one thing I knew to be true, my Zodar was never wrong.

Chapter 2

Tuesday, October 25

The next morning I went down to breakfast with a feeling of dread in the pit of my stomach. The note had said one had already died. Surely if the note wasn't a hoax the one who was dead would have been discovered by now. The previous evening, after I'd talked Ellie into picking up her dog Shep and spending the night in one of our guest rooms as a precaution, we'd headed back to my house, where I shared the note with Zak. Like Ellie, Zak had assured me that the note was most likely a prank, but in the unlikely event that it wasn't, we'd decided to bring the note to Sheriff Salinger, who'd promised to look into it.

"Any word?" I asked Zak as I let Charlie out before I poured myself a cup of coffee. Ellie, Alex, and Scooter weren't down yet.

"I called Salinger when I first got up. He assured me no one has turned up dead. He sent the note to the lab in Bryton

Lake just in case a body is found at some point, but he seemed to agree that the note is most likely a prank."

"I guess it's a good sign there isn't a body. It does make it seem more likely the note is a fake. If it's a prank it's a cruel one. Who would do such a thing?"

Zak handed me an omelet and a piece of toast. "I don't know. Seems like something a kid would do. I talked to Levi yesterday and he said the kids at the high school are all wound up with the big game around the corner."

"Yeah, but why pick on me? I'm not a supporter of the opposing team."

"No, but you *are* known in the area as being somewhat of an amateur sleuth and it *is* almost Halloween, in addition to the big game being just around the corner. Chances are someone saw you sitting in Rosie's last night and decided to have some fun at your expense. I wouldn't worry about it."

"I guess." I yawned as I let Charlie back in.

"So what does your day look like today?"

"I have the events committee meeting this morning and then I'm planning to head into work. Tiffany has to leave early, so I'll be at the Zoo until five. After that

I'm picking Ellie up at the boathouse and we're going out to the haunted house to help Levi decorate. He has football practice until five, so we should all get there at about the same time. I thought I'd pick up some sandwiches. Do you want to come and help? I'm sure my mom would watch the kids."

"I'd love to help. I should be done at the Academy at around five as well. I plan to pick up Scooter when he gets out of school at three and then drop him at soccer. Alex and I will both be done at the Academy by five, and Scooter finishes soccer at the same time, so we'll pick him up and then I'll drop the kids at your parents' if you can arrange it. I'll want to change clothes before heading out to decorate, so I'll just meet you here."

"Sounds like we have a plan. It'll be easier when Jeremy is back at work next week. I can go back to carting the kids around and you can go back to running the Academy."

"It has been a little crazy the past couple of weeks, but we're handling it. Other than your upsetting note, how was your night out with Ellie?"

"It was okay." I looked behind myself to make sure neither she nor one of the kids had wandered downstairs. "She still hasn't told Levi about the baby and that's beginning to concern me." Zak was the only other person who knew Ellie's secret. "I get why she's scared. I'm scared too."

"Why are you scared?"

"I'm scared that once Levi knows the result of his brief moment of indiscretion, the best friend triad will be beyond saving. I really don't know how I'm going to deal with that, so there's a part of me that's nervous for Ellie to share her secret. But keeping the secret much longer isn't going to be an option. She's starting to show and eventually someone is going to notice."

"The longer she waits the harder it's going to be."

"I know. She said she'd talk to him after the game, so I guess we'll just have to wait and see. Hopefully it will all be out in the open before Halloween and we won't have to walk on eggshells the entire weekend. To be honest, all the waiting is turning me into a bit of a wreck."

"I doubt you'll have to wait much longer. If Ellie doesn't work up the courage to talk to Levi pretty soon I have a feeling Levi and everyone else will figure it out on their own."

"I did point that out to her. Listen: while we're on the subject of Ellie, if my grandfather agrees to let us do it, what would you think about building an addition onto the boathouse?"

Zak took a sip of his coffee. "You're thinking of building an extra bedroom for the baby?"

"Actually, I was thinking about building a couple of bedrooms and a second bath downstairs. That loft is so tiny, and it doesn't make sense to have to carry a baby up and down those steep stairs. Ellie told me she's thinking about looking for a bigger place after the baby comes, but I really love having her so close. Besides, if she moved out we'd need to rent to someone else or return it to my grandfather to sell, and both of those options are depressing."

Zak paused as he appeared to be considering my request. "I think an addition would work well. The boathouse is on a large, flat piece of property, so it shouldn't be a problem. The kitchen and living area is basically one large room. It wouldn't be hard to build a wing off the living room. In fact, we might want to enlarge the living area while we're at it. Why don't you just ask your grandfather to sell us the property? We probably should have bought it from him a long time ago. If we own the parcel that'll make the remodel easier."

I reached over and hugged Zak. "You know I love you so, so much."

Zak kissed me on the forehead. "And you know I love you too."

I sat back and returned to my breakfast, which, by the way, was delicious.

"Did you find a costume for the party?" Zak asked me.

"No. I spent the whole time trying to help Ellie find something. I'll go back sometime later this week. Do you know if Alex has decided about the dance?"

Zimmerman Academy was holding a Halloween dance on October 28, but Alex wasn't sure she wanted to go. I really hoped she would. I knew she'd have fun and she both knew and got along well with the other kids, but she was the youngest student at the Academy by two years and had shared with me that she felt out of place in social situations. Ensuring that she'd fit in was one of the main reasons Zak and I had started the school in the first place. The problem was, due to the short building season that resulted from our heavy winters, we'd elected to start out small, with only high school students to begin with. Alex was more than capable of keeping up with the others academically, but she was only twelve, and the student closest to her in age was fourteen.

"She still can't decide," Zak answered. "I've tried to talk her into it, the other kids have tried to talk her into it; maybe you can talk to her."

"I will. In fact, I should go wake everyone up. If she isn't too groggy I'll see what I can find out."

Zak started breakfast for the rest of the Zimmerman crew. I could hear Ellie in the bathroom and I'd passed Shep on the stairs, so I knew she was up. I went in to Scooter's room and turned on his television, which helped him wake in a slow, even way, and then headed to Alex's.

"Wake up, sleepyhead," I said cheerily as I moved the cats who slept with Alex to the floor to make room for me to sit.

"I'm awake." Alex yawned. "Did you have fun with Ellie last night?"

"I did. We had so much fun that she spent the night. Zak is making breakfast for everyone, so you'll need to hurry and get dressed."

"Okay." Alex rolled out of bed and plodded over to the closet.

"When I was at the costume shop last night I wondered if you'd decided to go to the Halloween dance. If you're going, we'll need to get you a costume before they all get picked over."

"I know I need to decide. I want to go and everyone wants me to go, but it's turned into kind of a date thing."

"I see. And there isn't anyone you want to go with?"

Alex pulled a green sweater out of the closet to go with the new jeans she'd already laid out on the bed. "No. There is. It's just that..."

"He hasn't asked you," I realized.

"I get it. I'm twelve and he's fourteen. It makes sense that he would want to take one of the older girls."

"Has he asked one of them?"

Alex opened her drawer and began to dig for socks. "No. Not yet."

"Twelve is a little young to date, but if this boy hasn't asked anyone yet, maybe you can go as friends. You are friends?"

"Yes. Best friends."

"Is it Tony?"

Alex blushed.

"Maybe you can casually mention to him that you're thinking of going to the dance and ask him if he'd like a ride. If he has other plans at least you'll know, and if he does want to go with you but is too shy to ask you'll be giving him an opening."

Alex sat down on the bed next to me. "You think I should ask him?"

"Not in a datelike way. Just casually. You know, something like 'I'm going; if you're going, do you want to hang?'"

Alex lay her head on my shoulder. "This growing-up stuff is complicated."

I patted her head. "I know, baby. I know."

The Ashton Falls Events Committee was made up of ten community members who met weekly to plan and implement activities geared toward bringing tourists up the mountain to spend their hard-earned dollars in our small community. The fund-raisers also served to provide funds for community services and projects not covered by other means. The membership of the committee had changed a bit over time, but Levi, Ellie, and I were longtime members, along with my dad, Hank Donovan, and a few others.

"We need to make this a brief meeting," committee chair Willa Walton announced. "I have a busy morning, but with the influx of visitors who are expected this week for the big game as well as the Hamlet, I wanted to be sure we were on track for all the events. Hank, how are we doing with volunteers for the zombie run?"

"I think we're all set," my dad answered. "It took a bit of doing, but I managed to get more than enough bodies lined up."

"Excellent. And Levi, how are plans for the haunted house coming along?"

"We're on track. I haven't been out to the house yet, but I had Joey Waverly go by to check out the wiring yesterday and I plan to head out after football practice today. Zoe, Ellie, and a few others are coming along to help me get started with the decorating."

"Perfect." Willa smiled. "And the food vendors?" she asked Tawny Upton, owner of Over the Rainbow Preschool.

"We're all set. I have about half the vendors starting on Friday afternoon and we'll be at full speed by Saturday morning."

Willa continued to go down her list, asking for updates from each event chairperson. Luckily, everyone was organized and on schedule, so the meeting was short and sweet. As soon as it was over I said my good-byes and Charlie and I headed out to my car, which was covered with yellow leaves from the aspen tree I'd parked under. I love fall in Ashton Falls. The mountains are painted in red, yellow, and orange as the deciduous trees that cover the hillside change color. The temperature is normally crisp and cool, with slightly warmer days followed by chilly nights that make it a perfect time to curl up in front of a roaring fire with a loved one. We'd closed in our indoor/outdoor pool and stacked quartered logs on the deck near the fire pit in preparation for autumn evenings under the stars.

"Looks like that tree decided to dump all her leaves on your car," Ellie commented as she came out of the restaurant.

"I know. Isn't it pretty? I sort of hate to drive away."

"I don't know if you noticed, but that big sugar maple behind the boathouse is dressed out in full color."

"That always was my favorite tree. I'll have to make sure to take a look when I pick you up this evening."

Ellie gave me a hug. "Okay, see you then."

Being at the Zoo full-time while Jeremy had been on his honeymoon had been both wonderful and difficult. On one hand, since I'd made Jeremy a full-time manager and I'd taken on the responsibility of the kids and the Academy, not to mention all the amateur sleuthing I seemed to be forever getting pulled into, I really hadn't been spending as much time at the shelter as I liked. Being back full-time and really being a part of the everyday operation reminded me why I'd wanted to do this in the first place.

On the other hand, Zak had been doing double duty the past couple of weeks. Triple duty, if you really thought about it. While our principal, Phyllis King, was responsible for the daily decisions regarding Zimmerman Academy, and we had a full staff of wonderfully talented teachers, Zak still liked to have a presence at the facility on most days to oversee things, so when you threw in the software company he still owned and running the kids around town, he really did have a full plate.

"Thanks for covering while I was at the events committee meeting," I said to Tiffany when Charlie and I arrived at the shelter.

"How'd it go?"

"Pretty well. It seems like things are on track for Haunted Hamlet. We're hoping for a really good turnout this year.

Attendance was down last year after we had to shut down the haunted house."

"Is the haunted house ready for the grand opening?"

"Not yet, but we will be, although we're really going to have to work hard to get it open on Friday. Did the man who adopted that little sheltie make it in?"

"He did. I think she'll be very happy with him. I also called the woman who was interested in the golden that was brought in a few days ago. She's going to come by to fill out an application this afternoon. She indicated she'd be by at around three. I hope that's okay."

"That's fine. I plan to stay until five."

"I really appreciate your letting me leave early today."

"No problem. You've been putting in a ton of extra hours while Jeremy has been gone."

Tiffany shrugged. "I like to help out when I can. You know how much this job means to me. I feel bad leaving you on your own, but my brother is in town and I haven't spent any time with him in what seems like forever."

"I'll be fine on my own. If I have to go out on a call I'll just put a note on the door."

"The cleaning is completely done on the domestic animal side and I cleaned the bear cages, but Sunny was in a foul mood, so I decided to let you do the honors of cleaning his cage."

Sunny was our resident cougar, who did indeed have a bad temper but for some reason seemed to like me. I had no idea why, but when I encouraged him to transfer from one cage to another so we could clean or feed him, he cooperated like a house cat. When Tiffany made the same request he growled at her.

"Any new arrivals?" I asked.

"No, but I did receive a call from a woman looking for her lost dog. He's a little black Schipperke named Stefan who escaped when one of the neighbor kids left her back gate open after they went into her yard to retrieve a baseball. I had her send over a photo. I put a copy on the Web Site as well as the bulletin board and the desk. I planned to stop by the library, market, and post office on my way home to post photos. I encouraged her to make the rounds as well."

"Sounds like you handled it perfectly. I'll keep an eye out. We should probably let the woman know to drive through the campgrounds. All that food cooking over open fires tends to attract strays."

"I did suggest that. I also told her to post flyers in the bathrooms at the campgrounds nearest to her home." Tiffany began gathering her things. "If you need me to come in early tomorrow just let me know. I figure you might be late decorating tonight and want to sleep in or maybe take the kids to school. I might not answer my phone, but you can text me and I'll get it."

"Thanks. I'll keep that in mind. Are you doing anything special with your brother today?"

"He wants to take the paddleboards down to the lake, and then I think we're going to hike up Sunset Trail for the sunset. I haven't asked him about dinner yet, but I know there are a couple of places he likes to go when he's in town."

"It's a great day to spend at the beach. Have fun, and tell your brother hi from me."

"I will. Thanks."

After Tiffany left I put a note on the front counter that instructed visitors to ring the bell if they needed service. Then I put Charlie in my office before I went into the back to check on our guests. In addition to the bears and cougar in residence, we had a selection of squirrels, raccoons, and other small forest animals who needed temporary housing while healing from injuries. Scott Walden, our shelter veterinarian, was an expert at treating any kind of animal that came through our doors.

We only had a handful of dogs waiting for homes and had adopted all the cats we'd had staying with us during the adoption clinic we'd held prior to Jeremy's leaving for his time off. There were times when the shelter was bursting at the seams, but currently we had a light load.

"Morning, Sunny," I greeted the large cat, who had been hit by a car more than two months earlier. His injuries were extensive, but he'd healed nicely and I'd been discussing a fall release with the forest service. It'd be good to return him to his natural habitat before snow fell.

The cat growled at me, but I could tell after working with him for the past two months that it was an affectionate growl.

"Time to move over while I clean up." I opened the door to the small temporary cage and Sunny walked right into it, nice as could be. I closed the door so he could no longer access the larger cage where he lived most of the time and tossed him a piece of meat as a thank-you. I cleaned his cage, then returned him to it and headed to the front of the building to check the shelter phone for messages. After that I headed into my office to check my cell. There was a text from Alex, letting me know she'd talked to Tony and he was happy she wanted to hang with him. She added that I was the best mom ever, which made me feel happy but sort of sad for Alex's real mother, who was away on yet another dig and hadn't seen her daughter since June. Based on what I'd heard, Alex didn't expect to have another visit with her until the next summer.

I couldn't help but think about the sort of mother I wanted to be, not only to Alex and Scooter but to the children Zak and I eventually would have. I knew one thing for certain: I was going to be there for *all* the moments of their lives, not just the select ones that fit into my schedule.

I sent Alex a quick reply, then checked my e-mails. There was one from Clayton Longtree, the man I'd hired to trace my family tree back to the sixteen hundreds if possible. During my visit to Ireland the previous February I'd learned that I might be related to Lord Dunphy, the owner of the haunted castle where we'd stayed, via Catherine Dunphy, the lady of the manor in the sixteen hundreds, who I now believed gave her daughter, my ancestor, to the Donovan family in an effort to ensure a quality of life she might not otherwise have had. Clayton was making progress, but it had been slow. Still, Zak and I were talking about making another trip to Dunphy Castle over the winter. If nothing else, it would give me a chance to hang out with the castle residents, both alive and long deceased.

There was also an e-mail from my doctor's office, letting me know that all my tests had come back fine and there was no reason I shouldn't be able to conceive in the natural way. They reminded me that these things took time and I should just have patience.

Patience was sort of my problem. You see, Zak's mother had visited us the previous summer, intent on building a nursery in our home. At first I'd been outraged at the idea, but after giving it some thought I'd decided maybe this was a good time for Zak and me to begin to work on a family. I'd mentioned it to Zak on somewhat of a whim, and of course he'd been delighted. If I'd become pregnant right away I wouldn't have been subjected to all this second guessing, but it had been two months now and things kept happening to bring doubt to my mind. The longer I went without conceiving, the less certain I was this was the right time after all. I found myself feeling relieved when I realized that another month had come and gone with no baby.

I'd almost suggested to Zak that we wait another year on several occasions, but I loved him so much and I really didn't want to disappoint him. Still, we were both so very busy. Zimmerman Academy was now open full time and the construction on the dorms was finally moving along at a pace that would allow us to admit more students the following year. Zak's ward, Pi, was off at college, and Zak was planning to make a point of flying out and checking on him every few months, which wasn't a huge time commitment but would be difficult to do once I conceived. Zak had hired a full-time manager for his software business, but he was still in training, and Zak was still in charge of all new software development. Between the two of us, we really did have a lot on our plates.

My musings were interrupted by the shrill ringing of the shelter phone. "Zoe's Zoo; this is Zoe speaking. How can I help you?"

"There's been an accident on the summit near the Bryton Lake intersection.

A mama bear was hit by a car. The cub is up a tree."

"And the mama?"

"Alive but barely. She's being transported to the veterinarian, but we could use help with the cub."

I took down the location of the accident, grabbed my equipment, including my tranquilizer gun, hung a "Be Back Soon" sign on the door, locked up, and headed out. Answering calls in which vehicles were involved in run-ins with wildlife were by far my least favorite kind.

Chapter 3

By the time Charlie and I met Zak at the house and we picked up Ellie, the sun had set. The house Levi had located for the haunted house for Haunted Hamlet was really more of a cabin. Although it would be smaller than the ones we'd used other years, it was located at the end of a dirt road and was surrounded by forest, which gave it a feeling of spooky isolation. Dark clouds had rolled in during the late afternoon, creating an even darker night; they completely blocked the light from the moon.

"I hope Levi remembered to ask Joey to stop by to check the wiring," Zak commented. "It's going to be too dark to do much of anything if the electricity isn't on."

"He said he did," I answered. "I spoke to him yesterday and he told me he was going to leave the keys with Joey so he could go by after work. Joey gets off at three and didn't want to wait for Levi to get done with football. He was supposed to drop the keys back by Levi's when he was done, though Levi texted me today to let me know Joey had forgotten to drop the keys off, so he'd arranged to meet us here tonight."

"That worked out just as well. We could use the extra muscle carrying everything in," Ellie added.

"I think Levi has a group of volunteers lined up to help with the decorating," I assured them. "He mentioned that several of the guys had trucks and had agreed to help deliver props, although I don't know if he planned to have them come tonight or tomorrow night. He wants to leave enough time to get everything done, but given the isolated location of the house he didn't want to bring in expensive sound equipment and motorized props too soon."

"Is he going to have a guard at the house?" Zak asked.

"I don't think so. At least not until the weekend. We can ask him about it when we get there." My breath caught in my throat when we turned onto the dirt drive and saw not only both Levi and Joey's trucks but Sheriff Salinger's car as well.

"Salinger is here. That can't be good," Zak murmured.

"I hope nothing happened," Ellie said, fear evident in her voice.

"There's Levi now." I pointed to the porch as Zak pulled up and parked.

Levi joined us as we all piled out. I'd decided it was best to leave Charlie inside the truck because I didn't know what to expect.

"What is it?" I asked. Based on the grim look on Levi's face something *had* happened.

"It's Joey. He's dead."

"Dead?" I asked.

"Shot in the back."

"Oh, God." I paled.

"Someone murdered him?" Ellie asked as Zak put his arms around both Ellie and me in an offer of comfort.

"Looks like. Salinger said he's been dead at least twenty-four hours."

Twenty-four hours. That meant he'd most likely been dead when I received the note the woman had left for me at Rosie's. *One has died; others will follow unless you can stop it.*

"I thought you said he texted you last night to let you know he'd forgotten to drop off the key and he'd just meet us here today," I pointed out.

"He did. His phone is missing. Salinger thinks the killer is the one who sent the text in an effort to throw us off."

"That's crazy."

Ellie looked so pale. Like she was about to pass out. Levi must have noticed that as well because he put his arm around her and led her over to the steps, where he sat down next to her.

"Are you okay?" Levi looked into Ellie's eyes.

"Yeah. Just a little dizzy. Who would kill Joey?"

Levi shook his head as he looked at the ground. "I don't know. It makes no sense. Very few people even knew he'd be out here."

"Do you think it could have been a random attack?" I asked. "Maybe someone saw Joey's truck in the drive."

"Seems unlikely," Zak said. "You can't see the house from the road, so the killer must have intended to go to there. Although I suppose someone could have been squatting on the property and Joey stumbled onto them. Or maybe the house was being used for some sort of illegal activity, like drug sales, and Joey just happened to be in the wrong place at the wrong time."

"Of course if Salinger's theory is correct and the killer is the one who texted Levi, that would mean the killer knew Joey was supposed to return the keys to Levi, and he'd be waiting for them," Ellie added.

I looked at Zak. "So the killer must be someone Joey knew. Someone he spoke to before he was shot."

"Seems like," Zak agreed.

"Maybe Salinger's timeline is off and Joey texted me first and then was shot," Levi suggested. "The lights aren't turned on, which is what he came out here to do, so I'm thinking he must have been shot shortly after he arrived."

"That does make more sense." I looked around but didn't spot any obvious clues as to what might have transpired. "Should we go in?"

"Salinger said not to," Levi informed us. "He wants us to wait out here until he's done."

Waiting around wasn't one of my strong suits, but I decided to follow orders and wait with the others this one time. There really wasn't anything I could do at this point and I knew Salinger was a competent cop. Figuring out how and when Joey had died would be up to him, but figuring out who'd done it was more my specialty. Not that Salinger was incapable of solving the crime, but history had shown I was better. What we needed, I knew, was to make a list of everyone we could think of with a motive just in case the random-passerby theory didn't hold water. I kept a small notebook in the backpack I used as a purse and I grabbed it and rejoined the others.

"Just in case this isn't a random assault, let's start a list of everyone we can think of who could have motive to murder Joey while we wait," I said. "If nothing else it will help pass the time."

"You aren't going to investigate this, are you?" Ellie asked.

"Of course I am. It's what I do."

"After that weird note you received the whole thing makes me nervous. What if there *is* some psycho killer out there playing a game and you're the pawn? I really think you should stay out of it and let Salinger do his job."

"I second that," Zak added.

"Third." Levi looked up at me from his seated position next to Ellie.

I appreciated the fact that my loved ones wanted me safe, but there was no way I was going to stand back and do nothing. It simply wasn't in my DNA to do so. "There are several possibilities here. One is that some random person stumbled across Joey and killed him. If that's true and the killer is a squatter or a dealer using the property for his drug deals, the note has nothing to do with the murder; therefore, I'm in no more danger than anyone else. Another theory to consider is that someone specifically wanted Joey dead and followed him out to the cabin and shot him. That's where the list comes in, but as in the first instance, it doesn't involve the note I received, so why not look into it? A third scenario is that the person who left the note for me is some sort of a psycho playing a game and for whatever reason they've chosen me as their game piece. If the note is real, and if it is involved in Joey's death, then the killer specifically wants me to stop him or her. In any case, it seems my involvement is a logical choice."

I could see by the look on their faces that Zak, Levi, and Ellie all were about to argue when Salinger walked out, silencing us. He had a grim look on his face, which, given the situation, was understandable.

"The medical examiner from Bryton Lake is on his way up the mountain. While I'm waiting for him to arrive I want to ask you all a few questions, after which you're free to go."

"You know we'll help in any way we can," Zak offered.

"I appreciate that." Salinger paused and looked at each of us in turn. "When was the last time any of you saw or spoke to Joey?"

Levi jumped in and explained that Joey had picked up the keys from him the previous day so that he could come by after he got off work to handle the electrical. He further explained that Joey was supposed to drop the keys back at his place but had texted that he'd forgotten to do it and just planned to meet us there tonight.

"And what time was that?" Salinger asked.

"He picked up the keys around three-thirty yesterday and texted me at around six that night. I can check my phone for the exact time of the text if you think it's important."

"It might be."

Levi took his phone out of his pocket and looked up the time of the text. "Five fifty-two."

Salinger jotted that down in a notebook he'd taken from his shirt pocket.

"Did anyone report Joey missing?" Ellie asked. "I know he lives alone, but it seems someone would have wondered when he didn't show up for work this morning."

Salinger looked up from his notes before he answered. "No one reported him missing, but I'll check with the power company to verify that he didn't arrange to be off for some reason. Other than Levi, none of you have spoken to Joey in the past forty-eight hours?"

We all confirmed that we hadn't.

Salinger looked at me. "Do you have any new information to provide concerning the note you received last night?"

"No. When there was no body reported this morning I pretty much decided it was a hoax, so I didn't follow up. Do you think the person who sent me the note killed Joey?"

Salinger sighed. "I don't know. I hope not."

We all looked toward the road as we heard the sound of a car we assumed belonged to the medical examiner turn into the drive.

"I'll be tied up for a while," Salinger said. "You're all free to go. I know where to find you if I have additional questions."

Salinger went inside and the four of us, along with Charlie, decided to go over to Zak and my house to eat the sandwiches I'd purchased and to discuss Joey's murder. I knew the people in my life preferred that I stay out of these kinds of things, but I was pretty sure they all realized my taking a backseat was most likely not going to happen, so they might as well help out if they could. Zak opened a couple of bottles of wine while Levi built a fire and Ellie helped me make a fruit salad to go with the sandwiches. Charlie went upstairs to visit with the other dogs while we gathered around the kitchen table and served ourselves before I picked up where we'd left off with the suspect list.

"Okay, so number one on the list will be random passerby." I wrote this in my notebook as a sort of placeholder for the unlikely but still possible idea that the killer was a squatter or drug dealer who just happened to be on the property when Joey arrived. "Who else do we have?"

"Margo." Levi suggested Joey's ex. "Joey mentioned to me that he'd fallen behind on alimony payments he didn't even think he should have to pay because they didn't have children, and that Margo was on the warpath about making him get caught up. He said she was even threatening to sue him. Joey seemed genuinely stressed out over the argument the last time I spoke to him. In fact, he seemed almost irrationally angry over a situation that didn't seem all that impossible to resolve with a little communication and compromise. I don't know if Margo was as emotionally invested in the conflict as Joey was, but if she was I could see her being the killer."

Margo did have a fiery temper. I could almost picture the fire in her emerald green eyes, which seemed to flash in an eerie sort of way when she was angry.

"Of course if you're trying to get money out of the man, killing him seems to be counterproductive," Ellie pointed out.

"Unless he had a life insurance policy left over from when they were married or she knew that his will had never been updated and everything he owned would go to her." I wrote *Margo Waverly* down below *random passerby*. "Who else?"

"I know Joey has been drinking lately," Levi said. "A lot. One of the guys at work told me he'd even been involved in some bar fights."

"Bar fights? Was Salinger called in to mediate any of them?"

"Not as far as I know. Based on what Joey told me, he was just asked to leave the bar. Everyone knows Joey and no one wanted to rat him out to the cops if they didn't need to."

"In terms of these bar fights, does anyone specific come to mind as a possible suspect?" I wondered.

"I know he gave Todd Binder a black eye," Levi supplied. "There are others, but

Todd is the only one I can think of at the moment. I suppose we could ask the local bartenders who else might have been caught up in Joey's fighting spree."

"I think Todd is a good suspect. I'm pretty sure Margo is—or at least was—dating Todd," Ellie said. "I've seen them together a few times."

I added Todd Binder to the list. "Anyone else?"

No one responded, but I could tell everyone was still thinking about my question. Joey had taken his breakup with Margo hard. I had gone to high school with both Joey and Margo and I knew them fairly well, although we hadn't maintained our friendship lately. It seemed to me that both Joey and Margo had contributed to the failure of their marriage. Margo was a prima donna who seemed to care only about her own needs and Joey had tended to be irresponsible.

"What about the person who left the note for you? Maybe the reason they knew one was dead was because they're the killer," Ellie said.

I added *woman with the note* to the list. As sorry as I was that Joey was dead, I couldn't help but hope his death had been carried out by someone with a personal grudge and not some random killer bent on turning it into the first incident of a spree.

"Maybe someone should talk to the hostess at Rosie's again," Zak suggested. "I know you said she didn't know who the woman was, but given the circumstances maybe we should try to stimulate her memory."

"I'm sure Salinger will do that now that we have a murder that might very well be related to the note. Maybe the girl won't blow him off the way she did me."

Once we'd exhausted our list of suspects, which admittedly was pretty slim, I began to think about the haunted house. I wasn't sure how long Salinger would quarantine the place, but I doubted we'd regain access to it in time to use it for the Hamlet. I hated to bring up such a trite subject when a man we all knew had just died, but I figured we were going to need a plan B and it wasn't too soon to begin discussing it. I doubted we'd be able to pull together a replacement house with the amount of time left, but maybe we could replace the event with something else this weekend.

"I guess we should let Willa know what happened," Ellie said when I brought up the subject to the others. "I'm beginning to think we should just give up on the idea of having a haunted house as part of the event permanently. It never seems to work out."

"I guess you can add a *random person bent on stopping the haunted house* to your suspect list." Levi sighed.

"I doubt someone would shoot some innocent guy just to mess up our event," I said.

"I agree, but maybe we should look at the location," Zak jumped in. "I'm not saying there's a maniac out there who's so bent on stopping the haunted house that they'd randomly kill the first person who showed up there, but we've had the last three events canceled after a body was found. What if the killer chose that location specifically hoping we'd focus on the location as the motive?"

I didn't disagree with Zak, but I wasn't sure how to list it, so I just added *haunted house killer* under *woman with the note*.

I read from my list. "Okay, this is what I have. Random person in area, Margo Waverly, Todd Binder or some other bar fight victim, woman with note, and haunted house killer. Levi, why don't you talk to Todd because you know him the best, I'll talk to Margo, and we'll ask Salinger to speak to the hostess from Rosie's about the woman with the note?"

"I'll do some digging around into Joey's finances and whatnot," Zak offered. "There's a good chance we haven't stumbled onto the true motive yet, so it seems smart to keep digging into his life. I'm sure Salinger will do that as well, so I'll talk to him to coordinate. He seemed to appreciate my help the last time, and I do like to keep my snooping legal if possible."

"What about me?" Ellie asked.

"You look exhausted," Levi commented. "I think you should have an early night. Hopefully you aren't coming down with something. Come on, I'll take you home."

After Ellie and Levi left, Zak went to my parents' to pick up the kids and I took all three of the family dogs out for a walk. I was glad Charlie, Bella, and Digger got along so well. They were all so different in terms of size and temperament that it wasn't a given they would. Charlie, my little Tibetan terrier, was kickback and easygoing. As far as energy level, he tended toward the middle and wasn't as energetic as Scooter's dog Digger, a lab, or as lazy as Zak's Newfoundland, Bella.

As I walked with a flashlight along the lakeshore, I thought about the note I'd received. I wondered if I should be worried. There was no way I'd let Zak know how much the note had freaked me out or he'd insist that I stay out of the investigation and leave things to Salinger. The thing was, I felt responsible. The note had said one was dead and others would follow unless I could stop it. It seemed personal, like it was my job to prevent another murder. The more I thought about it, the more I wondered if the selection of Joey as the victim had more to do with me than with him. He wasn't as close a friend as Ellie or Levi, but I had known him a long time, and his death had acted as a catalyst for my involvement in the investigation of the murder. The thought that someone might be killing people connected to me freaked me out more than just a little bit.

I called the dogs and turned around when I saw the lights from Zak's truck pull into the private road that led to the house. I didn't suppose I was going to figure this out tonight, but I also didn't think I was going to get a whole lot of sleep. Maybe I should have left the kids at my parents'. Were they in danger when they were in proximity to me? One thing was for sure: I needed to figure this out and I needed to do it before victim number two met his fate.

Once we got the kids to bed Zak and I settled down with a glass of wine in front of a roaring fire. It was beginning to sprinkle outside, and the weather forecast showed rain on and off for the next week or so. I enjoyed the warm weather we'd been having, but some rain would be welcome.

"I received an e-mail from my doctor's office today," I informed Zak. "They said everything looks fine and we should be good to go."

"That's good?"

I glanced at Zak. The look on his face mirrored the question in his voice.

I wanted to bring up my doubts in regard to timing, but I didn't want to disappoint Zak with my on-again, off -gain enthusiasm for the idea. I really didn't know why I was so hesitant to move forward. "I'm sorry. I know I don't sound overly enthusiastic. I'm just tired, and Joey's death is weighing on my mind."

"He was a friend. That's normal."

"Yeah, but it's more than that. I keep thinking about the note. What if the fate of the next victim, if there actually is one, depends directly on what I am or am not able to discover in the next few days? If someone else dies it's going to be my fault."

Zak put his arm around me and pulled me close. "First of all, we're going to figure this out. Second of all, if we don't, any death that might result won't be your fault. It'll be the deranged killer's fault. You can't put so much pressure on yourself."

I wanted to agree but couldn't, so I didn't respond.

"Besides," Zak added, "we don't know for certain that Joey's death had anything to do with the note."

"How can we find out?"

Zak kissed the top of my head. "I don't know. Maybe the lab will find fingerprints or DNA or something to help us identify the person who wrote it."

"Maybe."

"We can't do anything about the note or Joey's death right now, so why don't we try to get our minds off it? Would you like to watch a movie? I downloaded the Halloween movies you wanted to watch."

"Yeah, okay. Maybe something funny rather than a horror movie." I leaned my head against Zak's shoulder. Halloween was my favorite holiday. I wished I could snuggle up with the man I loved and enjoy a movie, but all I could think about were the innocent people who might die if I didn't figure out what it was the killer wanted me to.

A half hour into the movie the sound of the doorbell announced a visitor. Zak got up and went to see who was dropping by at this late hour while I waited for him to return. When Zak did come back he was alone.

"Who was it?"

"No one."

"No one rang the doorbell?"

"Well, it must have been someone, but by the time I answered this was taped to the door and whoever put it there was long gone."

I looked at the envelope in Zak's hand. "What is it?"

"It has your name on it."

I took the envelope from Zak. My hands shook and my heart pounded as I opened it. I knew in my gut that the note was most likely from the killer. Inside the envelope was a single sheet of white paper with the words *Beware of a mirror that does not cast a reflection* written in black pen.

"It's another note in the same handwriting as the one I received last night. Are you sure you didn't see anyone?"

"Not a soul. I didn't see or hear a car. Whoever it was must have been on foot. What does it say?"

I handed Zak the note.

"Okay, that's pretty strange. What does it even mean?"

"I don't know. Maybe the killer is a vampire. They don't have a reflection, and it *is* Halloween."

"I doubt a vampire shot Joey."

"Probably not, but someone did. What should I do? How can I stop this? The first note referred to a second victim. How can I figure out who the second victim will be?"

"I'm calling Salinger."

I looked at the note again as Zak made the call. The script was bold and flowed in rounded letters. If I had to guess, a woman wrote it. I remembered the hostess at Rosie's saying that the woman who'd left the note had said a woman had given it to her. Finding the woman who'd delivered the note seemed to be the key to finding the killer.

"Salinger is on his way over," Zak informed me. "Maybe the person who delivered the note left behind some physical evidence."

"Like what?"

"A fingerprint on the doorbell or DNA on the note or envelope." Zak sat down and pulled me into his arms. "Don't worry. We'll figure this out. I promise."

"I hope so. I don't know what I'm going to do if someone else dies." I looked at the note again. "What do you think it means?"

"My guess is that the person who left the note is simply trying to get you to question what you think you see because what you're seeing might in some way be camouflaged or distorted."

I rested my head on Zak's chest. "If I can't trust what I see what can I trust?"

"You can trust me and you can trust your instincts."

Zak was right. Neither he nor my Zodar had let me down in the past, and there was no reason to believe either would do it now.

Chapter 4

Wednesday, October 26

I was sure I wouldn't sleep at all that night, but, miraculously, I slept like a baby. Unfortunately, that resulted in my oversleeping and needing to scramble to get ready for work on time. Zak had left a note saying he'd fed all the animals, walked the dogs, and taken Alex and Scooter to school. He hoped I'd have a good day and also hoped I'd leave the sleuthing until either he or Levi could be with me. Both Zak and Salinger had assured me that everything that could be done was being done to track down both the killer and the potential second victim. They also reminded me that the notes could still be pranks written by a truly sick individual who for some reason had inside knowledge that Joey was dead and decided to play a cruel trick.

Honestly, I doubted that was the case, and I really didn't think they believed it either, but it was sweet that they were trying to help relive my worry. And while my natural instinct was to grab the bull by the horns and not wait for anyone, I had no idea where to even begin to look for the second victim. I had a busy day coming up at the Zoo, so sleuthing would have to wait until evening.

Or at least that was what I thought when I left the house.

"Zoe's Zoo, Zoe speaking," I answered the phone later that morning.

"Zoe, it's Margo Waverly."

"Margo. What a surprise." Or was it an intentional coincidence? "I was sorry to hear about Joey."

"Yes, well, that's why I'm calling. Your buddy Sheriff Salinger came by this morning and asked me a bunch of questions regarding my finances and my argument with Joey about alimony. I swear, he made it sound like I was a suspect."

I sat down on the edge of my desk. I could almost visualize the look of indignation on the buxom blonde's face as she spouted her dismay at the quite logical turn of events. "I guess it's natural for law enforcement to question the spouse—or in your case ex-spouse—of a murder victim, especially when there was discord between the two of you."

"Why would I kill the rodent? I need the alimony he paid me every month, which is why I was so irate when the checks stopped coming. Without the income Joey provided I'll need to get a job. Can you believe that? A job!"

"A lot of people have jobs," I pointed out.

"Well, not me. I married Joey right out of high school, which meant I wouldn't have to bother with something so common as the need to support myself. I didn't want to work then and I don't want to work now."

"Maybe you can find something you enjoy doing."

"Very unlikely. So, will you talk to Salinger?"

"Talk to him?"

"Call him and tell him I didn't do it and to please leave me alone. When he left he was muttering something about needing to see life insurance policies and savings accounts. He's forgetting that I'm grieving and need my privacy in order to properly mourn."

I decided to ignore the poor-me speech and ask the question I really wanted an answer to. "Joey was murdered on Monday afternoon. Do you have an alibi?"

"I told the sheriff I was napping."

Based on the way she said the word I was pretty sure she didn't mean sleeping. "Were you napping alone?"

"Of course not."

"Did you tell the sheriff who you were napping with?"

"No. He didn't ask and I didn't say."

"Sheriff Salinger might not have picked up on the fact that *napping* doesn't necessarily mean *sleeping*, which is why he didn't ask, but I am asking."

Margo hesitated.

"It might get you off the hook," I said persuasively.

"Oh, all right. If you must know, it was the new tennis instructor they have over at the community center. I really don't want this getting out. The man might be a good tennis instructor, but he's not really my type."

"And exactly who is your type?"

"Wealthy."

I took a deep breath. Why had I never realized how self-absorbed the woman was? "I have no control over how Sheriff Salinger runs his investigations. I would suggest that you cooperate and show a bit more grief if you don't want to be considered a suspect."

"Like I said, I think I already am a suspect. He even had me write down some random words like *died* and *follow* on a piece of paper. I mean, really! What was that all about?"

Good for Salinger. He was trying to track down the author of the note. I wasn't certain he'd be asking all the suspects for handwriting samples. "Look, I can't help you with Salinger. If you're innocent I'm sure it will get sorted out. Now I have to go. I hear someone in the waiting area."

With that, I hung up. Margo was clueless, but I hadn't picked up on a killer vibe from her. Plus she hadn't gotten why Salinger wanted the handwriting sample, which she would if she'd authored the notes, and she seemed to have an alibi. I called to Charlie, who had been sleeping under my desk, and headed to the reception area, where I'd left instructions for anyone who came in to ring the bell.

"Tommy?" I greeted the tall, dark-haired man I'd had such a crush on in high school.

"If it isn't little Zoe Donovan."

Tommy picked me up in a giant bear hug.

"I heard you were going to be in town for the big game. It's so good to see you. What has it been? Five years?"

"'Bout that."

Tommy Payton had been the quarterback of the high school team when I was in school. As one of a dynamic trio, along with Joey Waverly and Levi, he'd enjoyed quite the level of local fame.

"I guess you heard about Joey."

"That's why I'm here, actually. I can't seem to get any information about what's going on, but I was told that more often than not you're in the know when it comes to local murders."

I took a step back and took in how good Tommy looked. He'd been a babe in high school, but with a few added years of maturity he was downright gorgeous. Of course he still couldn't stack up to my Zak. "Unfortunately, it's true that I do seem to get involved in the local murder scene more than most. To be honest, though, I don't know a lot about this specific case. All I know is that Joey was killed between three and five on Monday afternoon and his body was found by Levi last night at around five-thirty."

"How'd he die?"

"Shot in the back."

Tommy frowned but didn't respond.

"I know the two of you were close. Had you talked recently?" I wondered.

"No. Joey and I had a falling out when I was in town five years ago and we hadn't spoken since. I almost didn't come now, but I decided it was time to let bygones be bygones. I'd hoped we could mend fences, but I guess we'll never have the opportunity now."

"No, I guess not. Did you just get into town?"

"Couple of hours ago. I texted Levi, but I haven't heard back. I hoped we could meet up later."

"I'm sure he'd love to see you. He's in class right now. He'll probably return your text as soon as he can. We all need to get together while you're here. Maybe go to dinner or something."

"Sounds good. If you hear anything more about Joey let me know." Tommy pulled a business card out of his pocket. "My number is on this."

"Okay. Sorry I don't know more. Have a good rest of your day and we'll get together later."

I called Zak and let him know Tommy was in town and that we should plan a get-together. Zak said he'd like to catch up with Tommy but had some information regarding Joey that he felt we should go over as soon as we could manage it. We agreed to meet back at the house as soon as we both got off work. Tiffany had called to say she'd ended up having a late night and therefore would be late coming in, and the dog runs weren't going to clean themselves, so I made sure the note to ring the bell was clearly visible and headed to the back of the shelter.

I'd never noticed how much a baby otter looked and acted like an excited puppy until Todd Binder of all people brought one in that afternoon. Talk about a coincidence. First Margo called and then Todd showed up. It was almost like my suspects had gotten together and decided to make it easy on me by coming to me so I didn't need to find time to go to them.

"Where did you find him?" I smiled as the baby sucked at the bottle I held while he wagged his tail at a million miles an hour.

"Near the river behind my house. He was alone on the grass. I have no idea where the mom is. I looked around but couldn't find her so I brought the little guy to you. I knew you'd take good care of him."

"And I will. What a cutie." I could feel my heart melt as the baby pawed at my leg, as if to thank me for the meal. "He'll need special care for a few weeks, so I'll probably take him home with me. Alex is going to be thrilled to have a new baby to foster."

"I'm just happy I found him before one of our resident predators did."

"Me too. I'll call Scott and have him stop by to take a look at the little guy."

"I saw Scott earlier. Before I found the otter. He was helping to set up the maze in town, but he was gone by the time I went back by. He did say something about helping Levi with football practice. It seems the whole town is getting into the excitement surrounding the big game."

"Yeah, everyone really has pitched in. Did you by chance speak to Levi today?"

"No. Why? Is he looking for me?"

I set the baby inside one of the cat crates so he could nap now that he had a full stomach. "He was going to ask you about the fight you had with Joey. We heard his bar fighting had become a real problem."

"Yeah; he'd changed so much since high school. Seemed like he'd been going steadily downhill the past few years, but the problem that led to all the fighting seemed to appear a few months ago. The drinking and the paranoia alone were enough to make a guy want to avoid him."

"Paranoia?"

"Joey had all these crazy ideas that had absolutely no basis in reality. He came into the bar one night all freaked out that someone was following him. Another time he came right up to me and punched me in the face after accusing me of sleeping with Margo. Like I could afford to sleep with Margo."

"She's *charging* people?"

"No. That came out wrong. Margo wants to hook a rich guy who'll take care of her, so she only dates men with money. Young or old, short or tall, fat or thin, as long as you have bank she'll get in bed with you, but if you're broke, you're out of luck. She makes sure everyone knows what she's looking for so men without adequate assets won't waste her time."

"I see." I looked at the clock. I really did need to finish the cleaning. "I have to run, but before I do, can you think of anyone specifically who would have wanted to kill Joey?"

"Sure. I can think of three or four guys Joey pissed off. In fact, at least two of the guys I was hanging out with on Monday had been in fights with Joey over the past few months, but I was hanging out with them when he was killed, so I guess I'll have to assume they didn't do it."

"Can you think of anyone you weren't with who might have a motive?"

"You might want to talk to Clint Masterson. He didn't show on Monday, and he actually has the bank to have slept with Margo. I could see the two of them coming to blows."

"Okay; thanks."

Clint Masterson didn't seem the type to either engage in bar fights or sleep with women like Margo, but I didn't think it would hurt to have a chat with him.

I decided to let Tiffany lock up. She'd offered to because she'd come in late, and the cleaning and chores were finished, so all she had to do was keep an eye on the front desk until closing. If I left now that would give me a chance to track down Clint Masterson before I was supposed to be home for the evening. I decided to drop Charlie and the baby otter at the house before heading back into town. After speaking to Margo and Todd I doubted either of them were the killer, and other than Clint's, they were the only two names I had. Clint owned a car dealership and I hoped he'd be in that afternoon.

"Can I show you something?" a nicely dressed salesman with a big smile asked the moment I walked onto the lot.

"I'm here to see Clint."

"He's inside."

I smiled at the man and continued on into the showroom. Clint had opened the car dealership a couple of years earlier. Prior to that, residents of Ashton Falls had to go down the mountain to Bryton Lake if they wanted to buy a car. I wasn't sure how the dealership could sell enough cars to be profitable in our little town, but so far they'd managed to keep their doors open, and I'd noticed a lot more new cars on the road than I'd seen in previous years.

"I bet you're here for that yellow Mustang," Clint greeted me with a phony let-me-sell-you-something smile.

"No. My car is fine."

"Nonsense. You're married to the richest man on the mountain and you drive a two-year-old car? Cute young thing like you needs to be seen in something fast and sporty."

"I'm not here to look at cars," I assured him. "I wanted to speak to you about Joey Waverly."

"I heard what happened. Do they know who did it?"

"Not yet. I understand you and Joey had an altercation in recent weeks."

"I hate to speak ill of the dead, but it seemed like Joey had gone totally mental during the last couple months of his life. He was an angry and paranoid man who picked a fight with everyone he came into contact with."

Angry and paranoid. I was beginning to pick up a pattern. "When was the last time you saw him?"

Clint paused. "I guess a week or ten days ago. He came into the bowling alley and accused me of spying on him. Why in the world would I spend even one minute of my life spying on that guy?"

I frowned. "Spying?"

Clint shrugged. "That's what he said. The guy was mental."

Todd had said Joey thought someone was following him and now Clint said Joey thought he was spying on him. Seemed crazy to me, but then again, the man was dead. Maybe his paranoia hadn't been unjustified after all.

"Do you have any idea who would have wanted Joey dead?"

Clint paused again. I hoped he was considering my question, not just taking a minute to come up with some phony story to throw me off.

"I suppose if I were investigating Joey's death I'd have a chat with Albert Adams. You know he's in town? Has been since last Friday."

Albert had gone to Ashton Falls High School, the same as Joey and me, but he'd been a year or two ahead of us. He'd left the area after graduating and I hadn't seen him since, although one of his brothers still lived in town, so it made sense he might visit occasionally.

"Why would Albert kill Joey?" I asked.

"Not everyone knows this, but Albert was on track to get a football scholarship until Joey, Tommy, and Levi made the varsity team as sophomores and took over the bulk of the available playing time from the seniors who had worked their way to the top of the food chain."

"There are a lot more than three players on a team," I pointed out.

"Maybe, but the scouts are only really looking at the players who are flashy and bank impressive stats. Albert was the go-to wide receiver until Joey came onto the scene and took over the spotlight. His parents were broke; when Albert didn't get a scholarship he lost his chance to go to college. Now he works at a pizza joint in the valley. I ran into him in one of the local bars over the weekend and he was crying in his drink about how Joey stole his life."

"That's crazy. Joey was just a better football player than he was. If Albert really wanted to go to college, he could have applied for other types of scholarships or taken out a student loan."

"Maybe. Still, it seemed to me that Albert blamed Joey for his lack of success in life. I guess if you turn out to be less than you'd hoped it's easier to blame someone else for your problems."

I supposed Clint could be right. People who weren't successful oftentimes did look for someone else to blame for their misfortune. "Where were you on Monday afternoon between three and five?"

"Not that it's any of your business, but I was right here. You can ask any of my employees."

"Okay; well, thanks for your time."

"So about that Mustang…"

I glanced at the front of the showroom, where the car was displayed. It was pretty but completely impractical for mountain living. "Thanks, but I need a four-wheel drive with plenty of room for dogs, kids, and soccer gear."

"Boring."

"That's me. Boring soccer mom." I waved and left.

Clint was probably innocent, but it was beginning to sound like there might be something behind the paranoid behavior Clint and Todd had referred to in Joey.

As I left the dealership I called Salinger. Maybe Clint's lead regarding Albert wasn't as far-fetched as it had sounded at first. It had been twelve years since Albert had graduated from high school and it seemed unlikely he'd kill Joey after all this time, but at this point I wasn't willing to ignore any lead no matter how unlikely. Salinger was unavailable, so I left a message and then looked up the number for Albert's brother. His sister-in-law answered the phone and told me that he'd gone over to the high school to watch football practice. I called Zak to tell him I was heading to the high school but would be home directly after that, then returned to the car and headed in that direction.

I found Albert sitting on the bleachers, watching the boys run through their drills. There were several other people sitting in the stands while the boys practiced; luckily, Albert was sitting alone. I wasn't exactly sure how I was going to broach the subject of his rant in the bar. Unlike everyone else I had spoken to that day, I didn't know Albert all that well. I certainly hadn't kept in touch after he graduated.

"The boys look good," I said as I sat down next to him.

"I guess they're okay. Not as good as the team we had when I was here."

"I think you were two years ahead of me, and you're right, the team we had when you were a senior was one of the best there's ever been."

"Actually, I think the team we had when I was a junior was the best," Albert countered.

In other words, the team they'd had before Tommy, Joey, and Levi had been brought up to the varsity team.

"You know the Ashton Falls team made state last year?"

"I heard. See number sixty-five?" Albert pointed to the field.

"Yeah, I see him. I think Levi told me he's a sophomore he brought up to the junior varsity team this year."

"He's my older brother's kid."

Of course. I did seem to remember his last name was Adams. I hadn't made the connection. "I hear he's really good."

"Better than good. He's got that special something to go all the way. Feel bad for the poor senior who gets bumped out by a mere sophomore, though. It's a rough way to spend your last season on the team."

"I guess you would know. Seems like I remember Joey Waverly doing that to you."

Albert shook his head, as if he was trying to shake loose a memory.

"I guess you heard Joey was killed earlier in the week."

"Yeah, I heard. I wasn't a fan of the guy who stole what should have been mine, but getting shot in the back seems like a rough way to go. Did Joey ever get married and have kids?"

"He married but never had kids. He's divorced now."

"Can't believe the guy stole the scholarship that should have been mine and then never even used it. I heard he worked for the power company. What a waste."

I leaned forward so that my elbows rested on my knees as I looked out at the field of talented boys. "I guess not everyone dreams of going pro."

"Maybe not, but it seems like those of us who do have big dreams should have priority over the ones who don't when it comes to playing time."

I'd managed to strike up a conversation with someone I barely knew, but I still had no idea how I was going to work my way around to asking if the guy had killed Joey. An abrupt question in that regard would most likely get me nowhere.

"So, have you enjoyed your visit to Ashton Falls so far?" I figured maybe I could get him talking about what he'd been doing and get an alibi in a roundabout way, if he did indeed have one.

"It's been okay. Been a while since I visited, so it's good to spend time with the family."

"Are you here alone or are the wife and kids with you?"

"Never married. I do enjoy watching my nephew tear up the field, though. Guess I'll miss out on sharing that with my own kid."

"I don't have children, but I do have two kids living with me, and I know what you mean about kids' sports. I enjoy the endless soccer and baseball seasons a lot more than I thought I would."

"My brother's younger kid plays soccer. Went to his game on Monday. Talk about a hoot."

Soccer started at four, which meant Albert most likely was at that game when Joey was killed. I supposed I could verify that with the coach of the team his nephew played with. "What team is your nephew on?"

"The Raiders."

"The boy who lives with me is on the Generals. I think the two teams will play each other next week, if you're still in town."

Albert shrugged. "Might be. Haven't decided yet. Thought I might look up Tommy Payton. Heard he's in town. I hated him quite a lot when we were in school, but he used the scholarship he was awarded. I might want to see how things turned out for him."

"I spoke to Tommy today. He'll be around all week. I'm sure he'd like to see you if it works out."

Albert didn't answer, but it seemed like he most likely wasn't the killer.

"I should get going," I added as Levi called an end to the practice. "It was good talking to you."

"Yeah, you too. That cute little friend of yours still single?"

"Ellie?"

"Yeah, the brunette. Been thinking about finding someone to spend time with while I'm in town."

"Ellie isn't married, but she isn't really dating right now, so I doubt she'd be interested. There's a street dance on Saturday night. It might be a good place to meet single women."

"Not much of a dancer, but I guess I could just hang out on the sidelines like I used to do in high school."

"Could be fun. There are a lot of events going on in town. I'm sure you won't be bored while you're here. I'll see you at the game on Saturday, if not before."

I got up and headed for home.

Chapter 5

Later that evening, Zak and I settled into his office after we'd had dinner and the kids were settled down with their homework. I curled up on the sofa that was situated in front of the small fireplace that had been built into the corner of the large room. I pulled a comforter over my legs, which seemed to serve as an invitation for Charlie, Marlow, and Spade to all join me.

"So, what did you find out about Joey?" I asked Zak, who was seated in the leather chair across from me. He'd indicated earlier in the day that he had news to share and I was anxious to hear what it was. So far we hadn't heard of any more deaths, which I took as a positive sign.

Zak slipped off his shoes before resting his feet on the ottoman in front of him. "Several things, actually." Zak absently scratched Bella's head while he spoke. "I started off by looking into Joey's finances. It appeared he was broke, so I dug a little deeper and found out that he'd been fired from his job two months ago."

"Fired? Why? He's worked for the power company for a long time."

"The human resources department was reluctant to talk to me, so I called Salinger to ask if he'd be willing to follow up. Of course he was thankful for the lead and did just that. It turns out Joey had been acting odd the last month he worked for the company, and while they tried talking to him, in the end they had to let him go."

"Odd how?"

"Agitated and paranoid."

That fit what people were telling me. Agitation could definitely lead to fighting, especially when alcohol was added to the mix.

"Seems he filed several reports with his superiors about people following him or watching him from a house across the street while he worked. He was certain he was being stalked, but the problem was that he reported being watched from a bunch of different houses on a bunch of different streets all over town. His superiors tried to explain that it was highly unlikely that he was being watched from all those houses, but he was convinced he was being watched, and the more certain he was that he was being spied on, the more agitated he became."

"Do you think he *was* being stalked?" I asked. "I mean, he did end up dead. Maybe he wasn't crazy. Maybe he was right."

Zak adjusted his position before answering. "I'm not sure," he eventually said. "The fact that he was shot in the back does seem to support his assertion that he was being stalked, but there are other reasons—medical reasons—that could explain his behavior as well. Salinger is having the medical examiner take another look. We'll know more once he determines whether there might have been a medical reason for Joey's behavior."

"The fact that he was fired explains why he stopped paying his alimony, although I don't know why he didn't just tell Margo about the loss of his job. She seemed to think he was just flaking."

"As far as I can tell, Joey didn't tell anyone he'd been fired. We know he told Levi he was going to go to the haunted house after work, and Salinger spoke to his closest neighbors, who all said he left for work over the past month dressed in his power company uniform, the same as he had every other day since he'd lived there."

I frowned. "Why would he do that? It makes no sense. It isn't like he had a wife he was trying to hide his recent unemployment from."

Zak shrugged. "Beats me. It would seem that rather than pretending to go to work every day it would have been a better use of his time to look for another job."

"Which leads to the question of where it was he went every day."

"Salinger is looking into that," Zak informed me. "He figures someone must have seen him somewhere. This is a pretty small town and Joey was well known. On another note, Salinger told me that he's looking at Clint Masterson."

"I spoke to Clint. He said he was at work at the car dealership on Monday."

"Did you verify that?"

Actually, I hadn't. Man, I was slipping. "No. I didn't think to follow through at all. He said he was at work and I took his word for it. He didn't seem guilty."

"Salinger told me that he has a witness who claims Joey came into the bowling alley and accused Clint of spying on him."

"Yeah, Clint told me that."

"Did he tell you that he responded by threatening the man?"

"No. He left that part out."

"Salinger planned to have a chat with him this afternoon. I haven't heard how it went, but I wouldn't take him off your list just yet."

"I can't believe I didn't ask more questions when I spoke to Clint." I really was upset with myself.

"Don't be so hard on yourself. You aren't a cop and you haven't been trained in interrogation. Salinger is also looking at Kenny Brantley."

Spade got up from his resting place on the sofa and jumped down onto the floor. He trotted out the door, I assumed to head to Alex's room. While both Marlow and Spade spent time with me, they both clearly had decided they preferred to sleep with Alex and whatever animals she was fostering at the moment.

"Why does Salinger suspect Kenny?" I asked after Marlow repositioned himself to take advantage of Spade's absence.

"He was hired on full-time at the power company after Joey was fired. Joey thought Kenny was behind his being let go. He was pretty vocal about it. The day Joey was shot Kenny and Joey got into a heated argument at the diner where they both happened to go for lunch. Kenny threatened to use force to shut Joey up if he didn't stop slandering him."

I didn't know Kenny well. He'd only moved to Ashton Falls a couple of years ago and we didn't travel in the same circles, though Tawny Upton had dated him for a while, so I'd been introduced to him. I could see how it would get irritating if someone was going around town saying bad things about you, but to shoot someone because of it?

"If Salinger is following up we'll just wait to see what he comes up with. I'll add Kenny to my list and put Clint back on." I laughed. "Did I tell you Clint tried to sell me a car when I went in to speak to him today?"

"Your car *is* a couple of years old."

"My car is fine. He tried to sell me a yellow Mustang. What in the world would I do with a car like that?"

Zak grinned. "I think you'd look cute in a car like that."

"I don't go for cute; I'm interested in dependable. By the way, did you speak to the gardening service?" Zak had hired the company at the beginning of the summer and it had started off okay but had become increasingly undependable. "I'm afraid if we don't get the yard winterized we'll have an early snow and be in real trouble."

"I've pretty much given up on them. I'm not sure what happened, but they've all but stopped returning my calls. I'm planning to work from home tomorrow. I'll winterize the yard myself and finish decorating if it doesn't rain."

"Finish decorating? Don't we already have all the decorations?"

"I still need to put out Mr. and Mrs. Frankenstein and I bought some new pieces for the graveyard that I can't wait to try out."

I rolled my eyes. My brilliant, sophisticated husband was like a kid when it came to Halloween.

"Did you talk to Ellie about the food for the party?" Zak asked.

"We're all set. She's just going to make it over here. We have a bigger kitchen and I told her I'd help. She tires easily these days. I'm kind of worried about her. I mean, I know that women who are expecting tire more easily, but don't you think she seems overly fatigued?"

"Yeah, I've noticed that as well. In my opinion it's the stress of keeping her secret. Once the fact that she's expecting gets out and everyone including Levi gets over the shock, I think she'll start to feel a lot better."

"I hope so."

Zak got up and tossed another log on the fire. It was kind of nice hiding out in his office with him. Zak of course spent a lot of time within these walls, but I rarely joined him here because he was usually deep into cyber land. The office was both cozy and functional. The walls were paneled in natural pine, the fireplace was made of river rock, and a dark brown carpet offset the lighter pine furniture. One wall was lined with nothing but monitors and there was a glass cabinet filled with hard drives that buzzed throughout the day. On top of Zak's giant desk sat a keyboard and a smaller monitor for everyday use.

"I ran into Rachael Conway today," Zak informed me. "She was at the elementary school enrolling her daughter when I went by to pick up Scooter. She mentioned that she'd moved back to Ashton Falls, so I invited her to the Halloween party on Monday. I hope that's okay."

"That's fine. Did you meet the daughter?"

"I did. She's very mature and polite for a fifth grader. It seems Rachael has done a good job with her."

"I'm sure it's difficult to raise a child on your own, but Rachael always was the mature, independent sort herself. It's a shame the father isn't in the picture. Some guy is really missing out on a great kid."

Zak settled back into his chair. "I can't be certain, and I didn't really ask any questions at the time, but Rachael said something that led me to believe she left town when she found out she was pregnant, so the father never even knew about the kid. It made me wonder if he's still in town."

I thought of the brown-haired, blue-eyed ten-year-old and once again wondered if Levi could be the father. Of course there were a lot of men with brown hair and blue eyes in Ashton Falls. There might be any number of men who could have fathered the child.

"I spoke to Will Danner today," Zak said, effectively changing the subject. Will had been the math teacher for Zimmerman Academy until he resigned just after Christmas the previous year to move closer to his elderly father.

"How's he doing?" I'd liked the man and been sad to see him go.

"I'm afraid his father passed away over the summer."

"I'm sorry to hear that. I know he hoped to have more time with him."

"He chose not to stay in Florida after his father passed and resigned his position with the college he signed on with in order to be close to his father. He's been staying with a friend for the past couple of months. Anyway, he wondered if we had any openings."

I glanced at Zak. "You know how much I like Will, but what about Brady?" Brady Matthews had moved to Ashton Falls to fill the position created by Will's departure and had been doing a wonderful job. "I wouldn't want to see him displaced. He moved his whole family here and the kids love him."

"I have no intention of laying Brady off. He's doing a fantastic job and you are correct; the kids do love him. I wouldn't even consider bringing Will back, but he does have a much broader background than Brady, and he's done amazing work in theoretical mathematics, whereas Brady's specialty is applied mathematics."

"You're thinking of having them both teach at the Academy?" I asked.

"I'm considering it. Brady is covering the basic mathematics courses excellently, but if we brought Will on board we could venture into original research. I know that's a lofty goal for a small private high school, but when I think of the possibilities..."

Zak's eyes shone brightly as he spoke. I could see he was intrigued by the idea of charting a new course and he could certainly afford to pay two math teachers. Will would most likely be able to help Zak with the math related to his software development as well. There was just one problem as far as I could see. "What does Phyllis say?"

Our principal, Phyllis King, had dated Will briefly before he left town. I knew it had hurt her deeply when he'd moved, but I also knew she wasn't really angry at him because she understood his need to be near his father.

"She seemed fine with it. She was obviously shocked when I mentioned it to her, but after I explained my idea of having Brady continue with the classes while Will conducted original research on the Academy's behalf, she seemed really excited. I know we want to keep the school small so it's manageable, but if we could come up with some sort of breakthrough in math or physics it would really put us on the map."

I loved seeing Zak so excited about a new project. "I'm all for it if you think it's a good idea."

"I do think so. I think I'll call Will to invite him to come out so we can discuss it further. I'll need to talk to Brady to make sure he understands that his job is in no way jeopardized. I think he likes living here. He's commented several times how well his kids are settling in."

Brady's wife had died a year and a half before he moved in Ashton Falls, leaving him with three small children to raise. When he'd first arrived he'd seemed like a fish out of water, but Ellie had befriended him and my mom had gotten him involved with her toddler group, while Jeremy had introduced him around to the folks in his single parent group. Now that he'd married Jessica, Jeremy was no longer a single parent, but I doubted that would stop him from socializing with the people who had been there for him when Morgan was an infant.

I glanced at the clock. It was time I headed up to make sure my own "children" were wrapping things up. Scooter would stay up all night playing video games and Alex would stay up reading if I let them.

"I'm going to head up," I announced. "Would you mind letting the dogs out?"

"Happy to. I'll head up too as soon as I get the animals all tucked in. Does the otter need another feeding?"

"I'll check with Alex, but I'm sure she has that taken care of it. Did she tell you she's going to the dance with Tony?"

Zak frowned. "She's a little young to date."

"They're going as friends. Tony is a bit older, but he's a nice kid. I'm sure it will be fine. Don't give her a hard time. She's very excited and a little shy about it."

"I'll be on my best behavior, I promise, but you might want to talk to Scooter. He does like to tease."

"Actually, I hoped you'd talk to him. He listens to you, while he has a tendency to ignore me completely."

I got up and was gathering my things when the house phone rang. Zak answered the line on his desk. My heart began to pound when his smile turned into a frown.

"Okay, thanks," Zak said before hanging up. "That was Salinger."

"And...?"

"There's been another victim."

"Who?" I asked.

"Tommy Payton."

"Tommy's dead?"

"No. Like Joey, Tommy was shot, but his wound wasn't fatal. In fact, he called 911 himself. Salinger said he's in surgery right now to remove the bullet, but he's expected to make a full recovery. I guess the note was right. There *was* a second victim."

"Oh, God, Levi!"

"Levi?" Zak asked.

"The obvious connection between Tommy and Joey is football. Levi was the third leg of the unstoppable trio. It makes sense he's going to be victim number three if there is one."

Zak hesitated. "I don't think we should panic or jump to conclusions, but it couldn't hurt to call Levi and fill him in on the situation. I'll go check on the kids while you make the call."

Chapter 6

Thursday, October 27

I spent another sleepless night worrying about friends who didn't have the common sense to worry about themselves. When I'd called Levi all in a panic the night before he'd laughed it off, insisting he was sure he was in no way a target. He pointed out that he hadn't been part of the unstoppable trio for a very long time, so there was no reason for anyone to want him dead at this point. I tried to talk him into leaving town, but he reminded me that he had the football game of the year in two days' time and therefore wasn't going anywhere. He was, however, worried about Tommy, so we both decided to head to the hospital to see exactly what was going on. Somewhere around two a.m. the doctor informed us that, although he'd lost a lot of blood, no vital organs had been hit, and he was stable and should make a full recovery. By the time Levi drove me home it was almost time to get up.

Ugh! I didn't do well with only a couple of hours of sleep.

"Coffee?" Zak asked as he handed me a hot cup. I accepted it and drank it down before it even had time to cool. "Why don't you call Tiffany and tell her you won't be in today? Or at least that you'll be late," he suggested.

"I'll be fine once I have another cup of coffee and a shower. It's going to be a busy weekend and Jeremy is getting back later this evening, so I want to be sure all the cleaning and chores are caught up so he doesn't return to a mess."

Zak laughed. "You do know that *he* works for *you*, right?"

"Honestly, given the fact that he's pretty much running things and I just pop in and help out when I can, it sometimes feels like it's the other way around." I took a long sip of my second cup of liquid adrenaline. "Once I check in and make sure things are taken care of at the Zoo, I thought I'd go by to see if Tommy is up to having visitors. Maybe he saw something. I know Levi isn't worried that he might be another target, but I am."

"I planned to work from home today anyway. How about if I come to the Zoo with you and help you get your chores done, and then we can go visit Tommy together."

I smiled. "Really? I'd like that. And maybe afterward we can go see Levi and you can help me talk some sense into his thick head."

Zak frowned. I knew him well enough to realize I wasn't the only one worried about Levi. High school football wasn't the only link between Joey and Tommy, but considering Tommy was in Ashton Falls for the big game, things seemed to point in that direction. I'd filled Salinger in on the fact that Albert had been in town for both shootings and that he'd as much as told me the previous day that he planned to look up Tommy. I'd also made sure he understood just how angry Albert was that circumstances had derailed his plans for a football career and Salinger had said he'd have a chat with the guy.

I really did think that we'd find out that the killer had a motive having to do with the victims' participation on that long-ago football team, but I also supposed it would behoove me to look for other connections between Tommy and Joey. The two had known each other for a long time, which made it entirely possible they'd had something or someone else in common. I remembered Tommy had told me that he and Joey had had a falling out a ways back. Suddenly I was very interested in the reason for that falling out.

By the time Zak and I arrived at the shelter Tiffany was halfway through the morning chores. She informed me that the dog that had been reported missing earlier in the week had been found safe and sound, and that the new bear cub we'd brought to the shelter after his mother was hit by a car was settling in nicely. We chatted about what needed to be done before Jeremy returned and then Zak and I headed to the hospital before visiting hours were suspended while lunch was being served.

Tommy was awake and coherent when Zak and I arrived, but all he remembered was that one minute he was taking a walk along the lakeshore path and the next he was in the hospital hooked up to more machines than he deemed necessary.

"Given the fact that you were shot in much the same way as Joey, we're assuming there's a link."

"Yeah, that occurred to me." Tommy adjusted his position in the bed. I could see he was in pain, so I didn't want to stay too long.

"Do you know of anyone who would want both you and Joey dead?"

Something flashed across Tommy's face before he quickly masked it. "No. I can't think of a single person who would want either of us dead, let alone both of us. Who would do something like this?"

"I don't know, but I intend to find out."

"From what I've heard about Joey's death, we were both alone in isolated areas when we were shot. Do you think the shootings could be random based on opportunity or geography?"

I supposed it was possible the shootings were random based on location at the time of the shooting, not history, but it seemed unlikely. Still, in a small town you were likely to find a common variable between any two people if you looked hard enough, so I supposed it didn't necessarily mean anything that the two men shared a history.

"I spoke to Albert Adams yesterday. He told me that he planned to look you up."

"Why would he want to do that? He hated me when we were both in high school. In fact, he went to great lengths to let everyone know how much he hated Levi, Joey, and me. He blamed us for losing his starting position on the varsity team."

"He made a vague reference to wanting to see how your scholarship turned out. I guess that's sort of a lame reason to look you up after all these years."

Tommy frowned. "You think he's the shooter?"

"I think it's possible. Sheriff Salinger is looking into it."

"Albert always was a little unhinged. The fact that he blamed Joey, Levi, and me for intentionally ruining his life is crazy. We were just better football players who did what we were asked to do by our coach. I can guarantee you that we didn't set out to ruin anyone's life."

It occurred to me that there were probably other football players who were displaced when the younger boys were promoted to the team. If Albert wasn't the killer it might be worth my time to dig out my old yearbook to try to figure out who else might have a similar motive for wanting both Joey and Tommy dead.

"You mentioned when we spoke at the Zoo that you and Joey had had a falling out a while back. Do you mind telling me what your disagreement was about?"

"It was nothing, really. Just guy stuff. You know how it is. Broads and booze are never a good combination."

"You didn't speak to each other for five years," I reminded him.

Tommy shrugged. "It was nothing. Really. I'm getting tired. I think I'll take a nap."

"Okay. Please do let me know if we can do anything for you."

"What would you like to do now?" Zak asked as we left the hospital. Scooter was at soccer until five and Alex was going over to Ellie's to work on her costume after school.

I looked up into the sky. Dark rain clouds were making their way over the summit. By the look of things, we were in for rain that afternoon.

"Let's go out to the house where Joey was shot. I know Salinger and his men looked things over, but maybe we'll see something they missed. It seems, based on the timeline that's been established, that the killer was actually the one who texted Levi about bringing the key the following evening, so that means the killer knew Joey *and* Levi well enough to have gathered that information. I guess I'm hoping we'll stumble across a clue that will point to a link between the two men that has nothing to do with Levi. Maybe we'll find it at the house."

"Okay, but let's tell Salinger what we're doing. We need to work together on this."

Salinger was fine with Zak and me looking around, so we headed to his office to pick up the key and then to the house, which was located just outside the town limits, arriving just as the first raindrops began to fall. Based on the rapid drop in temperature and the increase in wind velocity, we were in for a doozy of a storm.

"This is really nice."

Zak turned slightly and glanced at me. "It is?"

"Sure. You and I are alone for the first time in forever. It's like we're on a date. A sleuthing date."

Zak smiled. "You know you're crazy."

"Good crazy?"

"Most of the time." Zak placed his right hand over my left hand, lifted my hand to his mouth, and kissed the back of it. "If this is a sleuthing date will I have a kiss at the end to look forward to?"

"Play your cards right and you'll have more than that to look forward to."

The rain began to intensify, so Zak had to release my hand to turn up the windshield wipers. I really wanted to find the shooter, but all of a sudden I was sorry this wasn't a real date. Things had been so crazy since school had started up in the fall that we'd barely had any couple time.

"I spoke to Willa today about the haunted house," I said as Zak turned into the dirt drive leading to the house. "She's of the opinion that we should skip the event this year. Based on her tone of voice, I'm pretty sure she's going to suggest we skip it permanently."

"I know the haunted house is your baby, but that does make the most sense. We don't have time to find another venue at this late date for this year's Hamlet, and it does seem that the venues we've identified as haunted houses over the years have had more murders than would be statistically normal. Maybe we should focus our energy elsewhere."

Zak pulled up in front of the house and parked. The dark clouds and increasingly heavy rain gave the isolated, deserted property an eerie feeling.

"We'll need to make a dash for the front door. It doesn't look like the rain is going to let up anytime soon," I observed.

"I'm ready when you are."

"Do you have the key?"

Zak held it up.

"Okay, let's go."

I opened the door to the truck and jumped out. I jogged up to the covered steps at the front of the house. The wind was beginning to pick up, causing hundreds of yellow leaves to fall from the aspens and blow through the air. Zak unlocked the door and the two of us entered the dark house.

"Are we looking for anything specific?" Zak asked.

"No. I just wanted to look around to see if anything stood out."

The house was sparsely furnished, with just a few old pieces that looked as if whoever the last tenants had been simply had left behind because they no longer wanted them. The structure had two stories, with a wooden staircase leading from the main living area to the upstairs, where I knew the bedrooms were located. I'd been to the house once before with Levi, when we were sent by the committee to evaluate its potential as a venue for the Haunted Hamlet.

My eyes gravitated to the dark red spot on the dirty carpet where I assumed Joey had been shot. We'd determined he'd been shot before he'd had the opportunity to fix the electrical system. If Joey had been shot shortly after he arrived the idea that his presence had disturbed someone such as a squatter actually held some water. Of course if there had been someone living on the property there should have been evidence of that as well, and so far, I hadn't seen anything to support that hypothesis.

I walked through the first story of the house, which consisted of the living room at the front, where Joey had died, a kitchen and laundry room in the back, and a small half bath off the laundry area. The kitchen was empty and covered in dust, although I noticed a streak in the dust on one of the counters that looked as if someone had set something down and then moved it.

The laundry room and bathroom were likewise empty and the living room contained two old chairs and a scratched desk. It really didn't look as though there was anything to find in the deserted house, but I decided to head upstairs to look around just to be certain. The stairs were carpeted in the same dirty pattern as the living room. Several of the steps had missing carpet, as if someone had peeled it away. I jumped when something crashed in the distance.

"What was that?"

"I think something hit the house," Zak answered. "The wind has picked up quite a bit. I'm betting what we heard was a tree branch."

The light from the windows had been adequate downstairs, but the windows in the bedrooms were much smaller, leaving me in an eerie darkness that had my heart beating with heightened stress. "Maybe we should have brought flashlights."

Zak headed down the hallway. "It's dark because the doors at the end of the hallway are closed. I think if we open them the entire second floor will lighten up."

Zak was correct; opening the doors helped quite a bit.

The bedrooms, like the rest of the house, were sparsely furnished. One room held only a bed, while another was furnished with just a dresser and an empty bookshelf. I opened the closets, which were mostly empty, although one did contain discarded hangers and another a stack of empty shoe boxes.

"I don't think we're going to find anything here to help us," Zak commented.

"Yeah." I sighed. "I guess you're right."

I looked out one of the dirty windows at the back of the house. I could see a light in the distance, most likely coming from one of the summer cabins that dotted the area. "We can check out that cabin." I pointed into the distance. "It's probably too far for anyone to have seen anything, but maybe someone heard something."

Zak shrugged. "Let's take one more look around here and then head in that direction."

The rain was coming down in sheets by the time we left the house where Joey had been murdered. The road that led to the little cabin whose light had caught my eye was nothing more than packed dirt that currently had tiny streams of water washing over its surface. I realized we'd best not wait too long before returning to the paved road lest the dirt one become impassable.

When we arrived at the cabin I saw a small white car in the drive and smoke coming from the chimney. Someone was definitely home. Zak and I hopped out of the truck and made a quick dash to the front door. This time the doorway wasn't covered, so we couldn't help but get totally wet. Luckily, the door opened after the first knock.

"Can I help you?" an older gentleman with short gray hair wearing a pair of fatigues asked.

"We're working with the sheriff's office and wanted to speak to you about the murder that occurred down the road," I volunteered.

The man didn't answer right away. He looked Zak and me over, as if trying to make up his mind about us. I guess it did seem odd that two people with no official ID would knock on his door in the middle of a rainstorm claiming to be working on a murder investigation.

"We really are who we say we are. Promise. You can call the sheriff if you'd like and check out our story."

"That won't be necessary. Come on in. We can talk in the kitchen. Would you like coffee?"

"That would be great."

Zak said he'd like some too as we followed the man to the back of the small cabin. The kitchen was rustic yet functional, if you didn't mind cooking on a wood-burning stove.

"Have a seat at the table. I wish I could offer to dry your clothes, but the cabin doesn't have laundry facilities."

"It's not a problem. We won't stay long; we just wanted to ask about Monday," I answered.

"I didn't see or hear anything, I'm afraid. I went into town to buy some groceries on Monday, though, and when I returned I noticed a white truck in front of the cabin down the way. I've never seen a vehicle there before, so I suppose that could be a clue. I mentioned it to the sheriff when he was here yesterday. If you're working together and he didn't mention it to you the truck must not have turned out to be significant."

"The truck you saw most likely belonged to the man who was murdered. He had a white truck that was parked out in front of the cabin. What time was it you passed the truck?"

"I guess around six."

So Joey was already dead. Darn, I'd really hoped someone had seen something that would lead to the killer. "Have you seen anyone hanging around the area? Maybe someone walking or riding a bike, if not driving a vehicle?" We still had some random person Joey might have surprised on the suspect list, but at this point I was pretty sure that wasn't going to turn out to be the answer.

"No. Not a lot of folks come out this way. Those who do generally drive. It's a good distance into town."

"What time would you say you left to head into town on Monday?"

"Guess around four-thirty."

"Was the truck in front of the house when you left to go into town?"

"Nope. Didn't see it on the way out, only on the way back."

Okay, that was new information. Joey had picked up the keys at three-thirty and everyone assumed he'd come straight out to the house, but if he hadn't been there as of four-thirty he'd obviously gone somewhere else first. The question was where?

"The murder victim was shot. Based on the timeline you've provided, it seems that occurred while you were in town, but the sound of a gunshot can carry pretty far. Are there other cabins in the area that are currently occupied? I know most of them are already boarded up for the winter."

"Guess you can ask the witch across the river."

"The witch?"

"I've never actually seen her ride a broom or turn a person into a toad, but the folks who live around here know she has certain powers."

"What sort of powers?"

"She sees things. Things that haven't even happened yet."

Suddenly I remembered the note. Could a very intuitive woman have been the person who left it for me? "Can you tell me how to get to this woman's cabin?"

"Just follow the road to the bridge and then take it across the river. Keep heading north on that road. You'll see the cabin. It's all by itself."

Zak and I thanked the man and headed back to the road, following the directions he had given us. It was almost Halloween. It might just take a witch to solve this mystery.

Chapter 7

Unfortunately, the cabin was deserted when we got there, though there was evidence someone had been there recently, so Zak and I decided to come back again the next day. After talking it over we agreed there wasn't much more we could do that afternoon, so we headed home. By the time we got there the rain was coming down in a steady downpour. Ellie was drinking hot cocoa with Alex, who she'd brought home after they'd finished her costume for the dance.

"Is Scooter home yet?" I asked.

"Yeah, he's up in his room," Alex answered. "Soccer was canceled because of the rain so his coach dropped him off. He said to tell you that they're canceling tomorrow's practice as well because it's supposed to rain for the next twenty-four hours."

"I'm glad they made the call ahead of time. I hate it when they wait to cancel something everyone knows is going to be canceled way in advance."

"The coach said we're in for more than two inches of rain," Alex added.

"Well, we can use it. I just hope it clears up by Saturday."

"I think it's supposed to," Alex verified. "Although it's going to make for a soggy opening day of the Haunted Hamlet."

"They probably won't even open the outdoor venues if the rain is still coming down as hard as it is now," I realized. "It's too bad. The hayride, the maze, and the pumpkin patch usually do really well on opening night."

"Maybe we should think about more indoor activities in the future," Zak suggested.

"Like a haunted house?" I teased.

"I guess you have a point about that. In spite of all the deaths, the haunted house does seem to serve a purpose. I should start dinner. Do you want to stay?" Zak asked Ellie.

"I'd like to. Thanks."

After Zak headed to the kitchen I asked Alex about her costume. I was glad she'd decided to go to the dance. She seemed superexcited about it now that she'd made the decision.

"I'm going as a pirate." Alex grinned. "Ellie helped me sew an awesome outfit. I even have a hat and a parrot for my shoulder, although I'll have to take the parrot off to dance because he's pretty big."

Alex's outfit consisted of a purple silk blouse with a black vest and black wader pants. She had a purple sash and purple knee socks with short black boots. The pirate hat Ellie had in her closet from a previous Halloween, along with the sword strapped to her side, made her look like the real deal. After I oohed and aahed over the effort, Alex headed upstairs to feed the baby otter before dinner.

"Have you found anything new about the shootings?" Ellie asked when we were alone.

"Not a lot, although it looks like Joey didn't even arrive at the house until after four-thirty, which is odd because he specifically hadn't wanted to wait for Levi, who got off at five."

"His plans could have changed after he picked up the key. Do you have any new leads?"

"No. Though we did get a heads-up about speaking to a witch who lives in the area."

"A witch?"

I explained about the woman who lived in the woods and her neighbor's assertion that she was a witch.

"Honestly, I hope she *is* a witch and I hope she knows something. I'm really worried about Levi. He is, after all, the third leg of the unstoppable trio, and I can't help but worry that he's next."

"I tried to get him to lay low, but he refused. You know how stubborn Levi can be."

"Perhaps if we can get him here in the flesh we can convince him that he might very well be in real danger," Ellie suggested.

"I agree a face-to-face conversation could help. Let's call him and invite him over. Zak is making pasta and Levi loves his pasta. I bet I can talk him into coming over."

"Tell him to bring Karloff." Karloff was Levi's dog. "He's more apt to stay longer if Karloff is with him."

Ellie headed to the powder room while I called Levi, who was happy to be invited to dinner. He informed me that his plans for the evening had been a frozen dinner that had been in the back of his freezer for an indeterminate amount of time. I teased him about his lack of a healthy diet and he countered that he doubted he'd be done in by frozen enchiladas. I imagined he was right about the enchiladas, but I hoped we'd be able to convince him that the possible threat to his health from the shooter was very real indeed.

"Is he coming?" Ellie asked when she returned to the room.

"He's on his way now."

"Have you heard anything new from Salinger?"

"No. I thought I'd call him to check in after dinner. I've handed him several leads he promised to follow up on. If there are names to cross off or add to my suspect list, I'd like to regroup before getting back to work tomorrow."

Ellie walked over and stood in front of the fire. I could tell she was trying to keep a lid on her emotions, but she still appeared to be fidgety and anxious. "Do you think if Levi is an intended victim the killer will go after him before the game on Saturday?"

"I have no idea," I answered her. "We just need to be sure the killer doesn't have the opportunity to go after him at all."

Ellie and I sat quietly, each with our own thoughts. I noticed she spent most of that time rubbing her stomach, as if trying to comfort her unborn child.

"It sounds like Levi is here," Ellie commented as a car could be heard from the driveway at the front of the house.

"Let's eat before we gang up on him," I suggested.

"Yeah, that's a good idea. He's usually a lot more amenable when he has a full stomach."

Zak made a delicious meal of spaghetti, meatballs, salad, and buttery garlic bread that seemed to melt in our mouths. We opened a bottle of wine for the adults while Ellie opted for milk with the kids. I couldn't help but notice the contemplative way Levi watched Ellie when she turned down the wine, but he didn't say anything.

During the course of the meal the conversation revolved around aspects of the upcoming Halloween celebration, which everyone was excited about in spite of everything else that was going on. I couldn't help but revel in the sense of hominess as my friends and family enjoyed a meal prepared and served by my husband in a room the two of us had decorated together. I loved the way Zak had strung small orange and white lights from the ceiling and the seasonal centerpiece I'd purchased from the florist that included pumpkins along with fall-colored flowers, adding a warmth to the already cozy room.

"Tell me about this boy who's taking you to the Halloween dance," Levi said to

Alex in a very parental and somewhat overly protective tone of voice.

"His name is Tony, he's fourteen, he goes to my school, and we're just friends."

"I've used the just-friends thing a time or two myself."

"Well, we really are just friends." Alex looked at me for help.

"They really are," I confirmed. "Besides, it's a school dance and there'll be plenty of chaperones, so there's no need for you to worry about our girl."

"What about you?" Levi asked Scooter. "Any datelike plans for Halloween?"

"Ew, no way. Me and Tucker are going to the Haunted Hamlet this weekend and then we're going trick-or-treating on Monday." Tucker was Scooter's best friend.

"Sounds fun. Will you be here for the party on Halloween?"

"After we get back from trick-or-treating. Can Tucker spend the night on Halloween?"

"That will be fine," I answered. "I'll call his mom."

Levi and Scooter engaged in a lively debate about the best Haunted Hamlet event while we finished our meal, and then the kids went upstairs to do their homework. I called Salinger while Zak did the dishes and Levi built a fire in the living room. Once we had all completed our tasks the adults settled in with their beverage of choice.

"What did Salinger have to say?" Zak asked me.

"He confirmed alibis for Margo Waverly, Todd Binder, and Clint Masterson, so we can cross them off the suspect list, at least for his death. Salinger doesn't have alibis for Margo, Todd, or Clint for when Tommy was shot, but at this point he's operating under the assumption that one person is responsible for shooting both men."

"I agree with the single-shooter theory," Zak said. "The incidents were too similar to have been carried out by different people."

"Unless the second shooter is a copycat who took advantage of the fact that there'd been a recent murder in town," I countered.

Zak looked at me. "Good point."

"I still have five people on my suspect list," I continued. "The random passerby, who I think we can pretty much eliminate because there were two shootings in two different locations; the woman who left the note for me, who we now assume left both notes; a random person bent on stopping the haunted house, who we can eliminate because that goal was accomplished with Joey's death, so there would have been no reason to shoot Tommy; Kenny Brantley, who seems to be out of the picture also considering the advent of the second victim; and Albert Adams."

"Why Kenny?" Levi asked.

"He was hired on full-time at the power company when Joey was fired. Joey thought Kenny was behind his being let go. I guess he was pretty vocal about it. The day Joey was shot Kenny and he got into a heated argument at the diner, where they both happened to go for lunch. Kenny threatened to use force to shut Joey up if he didn't stop slandering him."

Levi screwed up his face. "Seems like a long shot. My money is on Albert. He was mad when Joey, Tommy, and I made the varsity team and he's still mad about it all these years later."

"How do you know?" Zak asked.

"I spoke to him the other day after practice. He spent thirty minutes going on and on about how he'd had a bright future until we came along and ruined it for him."

"You realize that if Albert is the shooter and there's a third victim you're the next to be shot," Ellie pointed out.

"Yeah, I guess I am."

"If you're next on Albert's list he'll have to wait until you're alone," I said. "I suggest we prevent that from happening."

"I live alone. I drive into work alone. I'm going to be alone for at least part of the time every day."

"You can stay here and I'll drive you to and from work until we get this sorted out," Zak offered.

Levi looked as if he was going to argue when the doorbell rang. Zak got up to answer it.

"I really think you should take Zak up on his offer," I seconded. "Wouldn't it be better to be safe than sorry?"

Zak had a frown on his face when he returned to the room.

"Who was it?" I asked.

Zak handed me an envelope.

"Another note? You didn't see anyone?"

"Not a soul. It's odd. I got to the door pretty quick. You'd think I'd see headlights or hear the sound of a car leaving."

"Maybe the person who delivered the note was on foot," Ellie suggested.

"It's still pouring rain. It seems unlikely that someone was walking around in this weather."

Everyone turned their attention to me. I opened the envelope and read the note aloud. "*You have to know what to see.*"

"What does that mean?" Ellie asked.

I shrugged my shoulders. "I have no idea."

"Are we thinking the person behind the notes is the killer?" Levi asked.

Did we? I wasn't sure. If the person behind the notes was the killer it seemed likely that person was a woman, not Albert, who really made a good suspect.

"I think it's best to keep an open mind and look seriously at all suspects at this point," Zak commented. "I'd hate to focus on a single train of thought and then be wrong. In the meantime, I'd feel better if you both stayed with us." He looked from Levi to Ellie.

"I agree," I said firmly. "Karloff and Shep are already here. You can just run home to grab overnight bags."

"We can't stay here forever," Levi pointed out.

"True," I acknowledged. "But if the shooting is somehow football related, which is what I suspect at this point, whatever is going to go down will happen before the end of the weekend. Besides, won't you feel better knowing Ellie is here and not home alone?"

It took a little more negotiating on my and Zak's part, but eventually both Ellie and Levi agreed to stay with us through the weekend at least. I could see Ellie was concerned that it was going to be more difficult to keep her secret with Levi living in such close proximity, but the only way he would agree to stay was if Ellie did as well, and it was obvious her concern for his safety trumped any degree of discomfort she'd be forced to endure.

I went upstairs to check on the kids while Levi and Ellie were preparing to leave to pick up their things. Scooter had finished his homework and was watching a movie on his television and Alex, who had completed her assignments also, was busily writing in her journal.

"Levi and Ellie are going to be staying with us for a few days," I told Alex.

"Because of the killer?"

"Yes, because of the person who's been going around shooting people. I'm putting them in rooms on the first floor, so they shouldn't bother you even if they stay up late or get up early."

Alex stopped writing and closed her book, setting it on the bed next to her. "Can I ask you something?"

"Sure. Anything."

"It's really not my business and it's okay if you tell me so."

"Okay. What's on your mind?"

Alex bit her lip before she responded. "Is Ellie going to have a baby?"

To say I was shocked by the question was putting it mildly. I certainly hadn't said anything that would cause Alex to think Ellie was expecting and I was certain Ellie hadn't either.

"Why do you think she might be?"

"Today, when we were sewing, she kept putting her hand on her stomach. At first I thought maybe she wasn't feeling well, but then I noticed she'd smile a tiny little smile every time she did it. I still wasn't sure, but then her shirt hung open just a tiny bit when she bent down to pick up the scissors she dropped and I could see the top snap on her pants wasn't fastened. It occurred to me that she might be pregnant, but I wasn't sure and didn't want to ask her."

I was faced now, I realized, with a dilemma. I didn't want to lie to Alex, but Ellie's secret wasn't mine to tell. I sat down on the edge of the bed as I formulated my response.

"Sometimes adults do things that cause them to find themselves in complicated situations they aren't sure how to deal with. It's usually best to let them work through the issue they face in their own way and on their own timeline. It's also important to keep the confidence they may have afforded you as long as you're asked to keep it."

"So Ellie's pregnant, but she's too scared to talk about it and she made you pinky swear not to tell."

"Basically. But now that you've guessed you can't tell anyone either. Not even Scooter."

"I won't. I promise." Alex cuddled the baby otter, which had been sleeping on her bed while she worked on her journal. I wasn't sure where Alex's cat had gone off to, but I'd need to remind her that the resident cats might hurt the baby, so she needed to be sure to keep it in its crate when she wasn't feeding it.

"Has the baby finished his dinner?"

"Yes."

"Then I think I'll put him away where he'll be safe."

Alex handed me the tiny otter. "I know this is a dumb question, but how did Ellie get a baby when she isn't even dating anyone?"

I kissed Alex on the top of her head. "That, my girl, is a question for mature audiences only."

"I hope she's going to be okay."

I cuddled the otter to my chest. "Yeah, me too."

Zak and I settled into our room after everyone else had settled into their own for the night.

The fact that Alex had picked up on Ellie's secret due to her probably unconscious tendency to touch her stomach indicated that Ellie might have a problem keeping her secret from Levi with the two of them spending so much time together over the next few days. I'd have a chat with her in the morning to let her know what had occurred. But maybe it wouldn't be a bad thing for Levi to figure out what was going on. It'd take the pressure off Ellie to find the perfect time to tell him, and perhaps that would be best for everyone involved.

"Alex figured out Ellie's pregnant," I said after we got into bed. I sat back against the pillows I'd piled in front of the headboard.

"She did? How did she do that?"

"She picked up on Ellie's tendency to touch her stomach." I picked up the tube of hand lotion I kept on the bedside table and squeezed a small amount into my hand.

"Really? I'm not around Ellie as much as you are, but I never noticed."

"I'm not surprised. Alex is very observant and she spent the afternoon alone with Ellie today. I guess it makes sense that she'd pick up on the subtle clues. I feel confident that Alex will keep Ellie's secret, but it did occur to me that Levi is also hypersensitive to Ellie and her every mood and move."

After I finished rubbing the lotion into my hands Zak pulled me into his arms. I rested my head on his chest as we continued to chat.

"Do you think it's all that bad a thing if Levi does figure it out?" Zak asked. "We've both pretty much decided it's time."

"Actually, I was just thinking it might be a good thing if he figures it out on his own. Keeping this secret has been really hard on Ellie. She's stressing out over finding the right time and the right words to tell him. Maybe it would be better if the decision was taken out of her hands."

"It does seem that the ideal time for them to have that particular conversation has come and gone."

"Yeah." I sighed. "I have to agree. It's time. I do feel for her, though. Not knowing how he'll react has to be killing her."

Zak ran his finger up my arm. "He might be shocked at first, but Levi is a good guy and I know he really cares about Ellie. I think in the end he'll do the right thing by her."

"I suppose."

Zak shifted so that we were lying face to face. "So about that end-of-date kiss you promised me earlier..."

"Actually," I countered, "I think I promised you something even more if you played your cards right, which you most definitely have."

Zak grinned as he turned off the light.

Chapter 8

Friday, October 28

I woke in the middle of the night to the sound of rain hitting the side of the house. Zak was snoring softly next to me and Charlie was sleeping at the foot of the bed. I stepped over Bella as I made my way to the sofa in front of the fireplace, which still held bright orange embers. I tossed another log on the fire and then curled into the softness of the overstuffed piece of furniture. I pulled a quilt over my legs and watched as the flames from the dry wood began to dance in front of me. Charlie must have sensed my absence because he abandoned his spot on the bed and trotted over to join me.

Normally, I enjoyed the quiet of the night, but on this particular evening I found my thoughts in turmoil. I'd investigated many murders in the past. A number of them tied to people I knew as well as I knew Joey. It was always a difficult and upsetting thing to do, but this time, with the addition of the letters, it seemed as if the killer was challenging me to prevent further bloodshed. The only way to do this was to figure out who the shooter was and why they'd chosen the particular targets they had.

As I stared into the flame I reviewed in my mind the information we had to date. It seemed on the surface that the killer was the woman who we suspected was behind all three notes, but the reality was that the person behind the notes might very well be no more than a pawn in some psycho's game in much the way I was. The fact that two notes had been delivered to our home with no evidence left by the delivery person was beyond bizarre. Especially tonight, when the rain and resulting mud had provided a perfect platform for footprints, of which we'd found none. Of course it was raining pretty hard. Perhaps the footprints had simply washed away. I also suspected Albert could be behind the shootings because of the grudge he seemed to hold against Joey and Tommy, and he'd come right out and told me he planned to look up Tommy shortly before he was shot. Logic would dictate that both these people made fine suspects, but my Zodar was telling me that in the end neither lead would pan out.

Which left me where? *You have to know what to see.* What exactly did that mean? Was it intentionally vague and cryptic or was I simply missing something? Add to that the second clue— *Beware of a mirror that does not cast a reflection*—and you had a real puzzle.

The window next to the fireplace rattled as the wind slammed against it. I was somewhat surprised that I was the only one who had been disturbed by the storm. Zak was a sound sleeper, but both Alex and Scooter had knocked on our door during storms past and this one seemed to be as strong as any we'd had.

I snuggled Charlie's warm, comforting body close to my chest. *You have to know what to see.* I supposed there were examples of this; in art, for example. I remembered paintings I'd seen that looked like one thing but, if you changed your perspective, turned out to be something else entirely. Could it be that a change in perspective was in order? Initially, I'd focused on those who might want to do harm to Joey and then, after Tommy was shot, I focused on the similarities between them. The most obvious connection between the two men was their membership on the same football team all those years ago, but I was sure if I set that theory aside I'd come up with others.

Charlie growled as the wind changed direction and whistled through the house the way it did when it came down from the north. I held him tighter and whispered that things would be okay and there was no need for him to leap into guard-dog duty. Charlie was the sort to be alert and attuned to noises in his environment. At the time the third note had been delivered that evening there had been five dogs in the house. It really was odd that none of them had heard anything. Normally, all three of our dogs are barking in unison long before the sound of the doorbell alerted us to a visitor. Of course it had been raining and quite windy, which brought its own kind of noise.

"You okay?" Zak asked from the bed. He was leaning up on one elbow, looking in my direction.

"Yeah. Couldn't sleep. I guess I have a lot on my mind."

"Do you want to talk? I can get up."

"No. I'll come back to bed." I stood up with Charlie in my arms and walked across the room to the bed. "I don't suppose I'm going to figure anything out tonight."

Charlie resumed his spot at the foot of the bed and Zak wrapped me up tightly in his strong arms. No matter how loud the world yelled, I found I could always find peace and comfort in the arms of the man I loved. I closed my eyes and willed myself to relax as Zak's soft snoring serenaded me into the land of dreams and possibilities.

"Morning, sleepyhead." Zak woke me with a large cup of coffee.

"Sounds like it's still raining." I pulled myself into a seated positon and accepted the cup.

"It is. As far as I can tell, it hasn't let up at all."

"Even if the rain lets up by tomorrow the field is going to be a soggy mess."

"Mud and football do seem to go together. I'm going to take the kids to school and then I'll be back. Levi has already gone and Ellie is still sleeping."

"I thought you were going to drive Levi to work."

"He insisted on taking his own car, and he's a grown man. He'll be fine. When I get back we'll brainstorm. Maybe we can figure out what last night's note means. In the meantime, try not to stress too much"

Easier said than done.

"Oh, and Levi asked if we were coming to the pep rally this morning," Zak added. "I told him I'd ask you."

I enjoyed the pep rallies the high school held before each game. "I wouldn't mind going."

"It's at eleven. Maybe we can do lunch afterward."

After Zak left I settled back against my pillows with my coffee. I was sorry the rain was going to ruin opening day for Haunted Hamlet, but I did enjoy listening to the sound of the rain hitting the window. It made me think of our trip to Ireland, when it rained almost the entire time we were there. I'd been thinking a lot about another trip to Dunphy Castle. Maybe after we solved this murder and got through the weekend activities I'd do something about making more specific plans.

Jeremy had returned from his honeymoon the previous evening. He'd called to say he was back and that he'd had a wonderful time. Initially, he hadn't been due to return to work until the following week, but he'd said he'd missed hanging out with the animals and was ready to get back to his regular routine, so he planned to be back at the shelter first thing this morning. Given the current situation, it was just as well he was back at the helm at the Zoo, freeing me up to focus on finding the killer.

I was debating whether to head downstairs for more coffee or skip it in favor of a hot shower when the phone rang. It was Salinger.

"Donovan. I have news, and fairly interesting news at that."

I yawned. "Okay, what's your news?"

"It appears Joey Waverly and Tommy Payton may have been shot by different people."

That got my attention. "What?"

"At this point we don't know that for certain, but we do know they were shot with different guns."

"Okay, that's just bizarre. Are you sure?"

"Of course I'm sure."

Salinger sounded tired and frustrated, and I could understand that. He was, after all, the person responsible for putting an end to this very strange shooting spree, and I was sure he was getting a lot of pressure to do just that from the main office in Bryton Lake.

"Zak and I have a few things we want to follow up on. I'm not sure our leads will end up anywhere, but we'll keep you in the loop. If there are two shooters we may be looking at a whole different set of motives."

Salinger sighed. "You know I appreciate your help. If you find out anything that might help us nail this down call me. Just be careful."

"Yeah, we will."

I decided to skip the coffee and head for the shower. I had no idea how this piece of news would help or hinder us, but I wanted to be up and dressed when Zak returned in the event he had some insight he wanted to follow up on before the pep rally. Two shooters? Wow. That really would be a game changer if it ended up being true.

When I got downstairs I found a note from Ellie, saying that she and Shep had headed home. She had a dentist's appointment that day and wanted to shower and change beforehand. She reminded me that the only reason she'd stayed the previous night was so that Levi would, and that she herself wasn't considered to be a potential victim, so I shouldn't worry. Of course if there were two killers and the shootings were unrelated, Levi might not be a potential victim either. But with such a wild card thrown into the deck, it was hard to know who might be next.

"I half-expected to find you still in bed," Zak said when he walked into the kitchen through the side door, which led out to the drive. He took off his coat and hung it on a peg, then shook the rain from his hair.

"Salinger called. It looks like Joey and Tommy were shot with different guns. Salinger is now entertaining the idea of two shooters."

Zak frowned. "Two shooters? That makes no sense."

"Agreed. I think Salinger is pretty frustrated with the whole thing."

"I can see why. Two shooters would change everything."

Zak poured himself a cup of coffee before walking across the room and opening the refrigerator. "Eggs?"

"Not if we're going to lunch after the rally. Maybe just cereal."

Zak grabbed the milk as well as a box of bran flakes. He set the ingredients on the table while I took out two bowls.

"I was thinking about going back to the house the neighbor identified as the witch's," I added. "I'm not saying the woman is a witch, but it would really help if someone saw something. I'm about out of suspects, although if there are two shooters I guess we can add a random person back onto the list. The only reason we eliminated him was because a random person wouldn't be responsible for Tommy's shooting as well."

"I'm in," Zak answered. "We might want to go by to talk to Tommy again as well. Now that he's had a chance to recover a bit maybe he remembers something. Anything at all could help."

"Yeah, okay. That sounds like a good plan. I just need to check on the baby otter before we go. I'm sure Alex fed him this morning, but it's going to be a long day and I don't want to forget about the little guy."

When we arrived at the little cabin that had been pointed out as the witch's, I was glad to see a curl of smoke rising from the chimney. Zak and I parked in front of it and then hurried to the front door, which was elevated just a bit off the wet, muddy ground. The rain had slowed to a drizzle and I hoped it would stop altogether within the next couple of hours.

"Yes?" a short, gnarled woman with white hair and a hunched back asked.

"My name is Zoe and this is Zak. We're consultants with the sheriff's office and we wanted to ask you about the shooting that occurred at the house down the road earlier in the week. Do you think we could come in for a few minutes?"

"You must be here to see Yari. She's been expecting you." The woman took a step back and motioned for us to enter the small but tidy living area.

"Yari?" I asked.

"My daughter. Have a seat. I'm sure she'll be down any minute."

I glanced toward the stairs, which I assumed led to bedrooms. The cabin seemed to be compact but functional. Zak took my hand and led me over to the sofa, which was situated along one wall. I didn't notice where the old woman had gone off to. She was there one minute and then she was gone. I supposed she must have slipped upstairs while I wasn't looking.

I looked around the nicely decorated room. There were flowers on the tables, as well as a variety of photos displayed on almost every available surface. There was one in particular that caught my eye, of a beautiful woman with long black hair and black, or at least very dark brown, eyes. There was a contemplative expression on her face that led me to believe the photographer had caught her while she was daydreaming. There was a forest and a river in the background. It didn't look like the photo had been taken locally, but the location did seem familiar.

"I'm happy you arrived on time," the woman from the photo greeted me as she floated down the stairs.

I frowned. "On time? I'm afraid you might have us confused with someone else. We didn't have an appointment."

"No. I'm not confused. Tea?"

"No, thank you. We won't keep you long. We just wanted to ask about the shooting down the road earlier in the week. We were hoping you saw or heard something."

"*Saw* is such a tricky word," the woman said as she sat down in a chair across from us.

I glanced at Zak, who shrugged. I was beginning to think this woman was some sort of a nutjob who wasn't going to be able to help us at all when I noticed a letter on the table in front of me. The handwriting on the envelope looked an awful lot like the one on the notes I'd been receiving.

"You sent me the notes."

"Yes. I assumed that was why you were here."

"I'm here because the man down the road suggested we speak to you. Why did you send me the notes? And why all the secrecy? If you had news to share why not just seek me out and speak to me?"

She shrugged. "There are those who do not understand the nature of my gift. They shun me and deny that which I have to share, so I have learned it is best to remain in the shadows until I am sure."

"Gift?"

She just smiled.

"The first note said 'one has died, others will follow.' I'm assuming you were referring to Joey Waverly and Tommy Payton. Do you know who shot them?"

"Joey is the one who died, but Tommy is not one of those who will follow."

"I don't understand. Tommy was shot on Wednesday. Are you saying someone else will die?"

"Unless you can stop it."

"Stop it? Stop it how? I have no idea where to even start. Are you absolutely certain Tommy wasn't the second victim you sensed?"

The woman sat back and looked directly at me. She seemed to be looking right through me, but she didn't say anything. The experience was beyond creepy. It felt as if she somehow had entered my body in order to take a look around. Personally, I prefer the space within my mind be occupied by me and me alone.

"The first victim, Joey, was surprised by what occurred. I sensed a lot of dark energy surrounding him at the moment he died. I do not sense the same surprise or dark energy when it comes to the second victim, Tommy. My sense is that the initial reading I received, which indicated that one had died and others would follow, has not come to completion."

"So someone else will die?"

"Perhaps."

"But I have the power to stop it? That's what you said. Right?"

"Yes. I sense you have the power to stop whatever it is that is destined to occur. I also sense your time to intervene is coming to an end."

"So what do I do? How do I stop it?"

"You have what you need to find your answers; you simply must know what to see."

Boy, did I wish this woman would speak in clearly understandable English and not in riddles that didn't seem to lead anywhere. "Yes, I remember the note from last night. It said you had to know what to see. I've also been thinking about the second note and the reference to the mirror. Are you trying to tell me that the answer lies in the perspective? Like if I look at things from one angle I see one thing, but if I look at them from another I'll see something else entirely?"

The woman smiled.

"Is there anything you can tell me specific to these shootings that will point me in a direction? Did you see or hear anything on the night Joey was murdered? Anything at all?"

She stood up. "I'm sorry. I've told you what I can. Sometimes the answer lies not in the image before you but in the empty spaces."

"What do you think?" Zak asked as we headed back into town.

"I don't know. Part of me thinks she's just a kook and another feels like what she says makes perfect sense. If she's correct that Tommy isn't the one who follows from the first note, I'm back to being freaked out about Levi being the next victim."

"She never said Levi was in any danger," Zak pointed out.

"That's true. I guess it just feels like he would be the one to follow based on what we know about Tommy and Joey. If Salinger is right and there are two shooters, though, everything we think we know is moot."

"Maybe Tommy remembers who shot him now that he's had some time to think about it," Zak said again.

"Maybe. Let's head there next."

When we arrived at the hospital we learned Tommy had checked himself out earlier that morning.

"What do you mean, he checked himself out?" I asked the nurse. "He was shot just two days ago. There was no way he was ready to be discharged."

"I agree. The doctor agreed. Mr. Payton left against doctor's orders. While it was an unwise choice, it was one he was free to make."

"Do you know where he went?"

"I'm afraid I don't. Now, if you'll excuse me, I have patients to see to."

I looked at Zak. "What in the world is going on?"

"I wish I knew. I wonder if Salinger knows about Tommy."

"Let's head over to his office. If he's there we can compare notes before the rally."

As it turned out, Salinger hadn't been aware that Tommy had left the hospital. "Seems suspicious that the man would check himself out when he clearly needed to be there just hours after we discovered there were two different guns used in the shootings."

"You think Tommy knows something about one or both of the shootings that he doesn't want to share?" I asked him.

"Seems like he's trying to hide something. What can you tell me about the relationship between the two victims?"

"They were on the same high school football team and, along with Levi, provided a force to be reckoned with. I'd say the three were good friends both on and off the field. Tommy left this area to go to college and never moved back. Joey never did go to college, and of course Levi went to college but then returned to Ashton Falls. I'd say by now they're more acquaintances than close friends."

"Was there any discord between them?"

I thought about Salinger's question. "They had their tiffs while still in school. I know they all dated the same girls at different times. I imagine that led to short-term discord, but overall they were really close."

"Do you remember the names of any of these girls?"

"Rachael Conway, for one. I'm pretty sure she dated all three of them in high school. She moved away shortly after graduation, but she just moved back to town a week or so ago."

Salinger wrote down her name. "Anything else?"

"Tommy did mention that he and Joey had a falling out five years ago that was never resolved. I asked him what the conflict was about, but he declined to say."

"Five years is a long time to stay mad."

"I agree. And so did Tommy. He told me the main reason he was in Ashton Falls now was to try to mend fences with Joey, but he died before he had the chance."

Salinger made a few more notes. I thought about mentioning that I'd met the woman who had sent me the notes, but for some reason I hesitated. I wasn't quite sure what I was going to do with this piece of information yet. I chatted with the sheriff for a few more minutes before heading to the high school for the rally, where we found that Ellie had saved us seats. Zak noticed a friend in the crowd and went to say hi while I joined Ellie on the wooden bleachers.

"It seems like the whole town is pumped up for the big game," Ellie commented as I settled in.

"It is a big game. State champion two years in a row would be quite an accomplishment. I wonder if Levi has all his players available for the game. As of last week two of his starters were out for medical reasons."

"He told me last night that he had the full team back for the first time this year. He's really stoked about his chances. Oh, look; there he is now."

I watched Ellie as she waved at the father of her child. I couldn't help but experience a feeling of déjà vu as I witnessed the look of love on her face. It was at a pep rally for the big game three years ago that I'd first realized Ellie's feelings for Levi had changed from friendship to more. At the time I'd been afraid her feelings would ruin the foundation of the connection the three of us had shared for most of our lives, and while so much had happened since then, I had that same fear now regarding her pregnancy. It was funny how much things had changed while not really changing at all.

"So I met a witch today," I shared with Ellie while we waited for the cheerleaders to begin their routine.

"A witch?"

"I don't know if she's a real witch, but she sure looks the way I always pictured a witch would. The friendly kind, not the scary ones. Anyway, it turned out she was the one who'd been sending me the notes."

Ellie turned and gave me her full attention. "Is she the shooter?"

"No, I don't think so. At least she didn't seem like the sort to go around shooting people."

"So why all the secrecy?"

"She wasn't sure I would be open to what she had to tell me if she just walked up and said it. You know, she's probably right. I most likely would have thought she was a nutjob that first night. She has an odd way about her that I really had to look past."

Ellie waved as Levi looked in our direction. "Odd how?"

"She talks in riddles rather than just coming out with whatever it is she wants to say. I still have no idea whether she knows anything or not. On one hand she has the look of someone with a secret, but on the other, if she knew who shot Joey and Tommy why wouldn't she just give me a name?"

"Are you sure she isn't the shooter and she's being vague to throw you off?"

"Like I said, I didn't get that vibe, but who knows? This whole thing has been so random up to this point." I lowered my voice, though it really wasn't necessary with all the cheering going on. "Did you hear that Tommy and Joey were shot with different guns?"

"Seriously?"

"Salinger thinks we might be looking at two different shooters."

Ellie smiled. "That means Levi might not be a target after all."

"If someone killed Joey because of some beef they had with him and then someone else turned around and shot Tommy for an unrelated reason, then yeah, Levi might be off the hook as a potential target. But the witch said Tommy wasn't the one who would follow, leading me to believe there's someone else who's still potentially in danger."

Ellie looked skeptical. "Are you sure this woman really has some sort of a gift and knows what's going to happen? The whole thing seems pretty weird to me."

I shrugged. "The vagueness of the messages she sent me make it all but impossible to verify their legitimacy. Right now I'm not going to discount anything."

"Okay, let's look at the two-shooters theory. What are the odds there would be two shooters with two different motives?"

"Honestly, not great," I answered. "The only thing I can think of is that someone had a beef with Tommy and used the fact that his old friend Joey had been shot to his or her advantage. We haven't even looked at suspects specific to Tommy. Once he was shot we all just assumed the attempted murder was related to his relationship with Joey."

"That theory actually makes sense. If I had a beef with Tommy copying the method used to kill Joey would be a perfect way to divert attention away from myself, assuming I wasn't related to Joey in any way. Do you have any suspects specific to Tommy?"

"Not yet. It's going to be harder to come up with suspects related to Tommy but not Joey because Tommy doesn't live here anymore and hasn't for quite some time. He only just got into town on Wednesday and was shot that day. Not much time for someone to plan to kill him."

"Tommy didn't get into town on Wednesday."

"He didn't? He told me he'd only been here for a few hours when I spoke to him that day."

"I ran into Stephanie Bird on Monday, and she told me she'd had drinks with Tommy over the weekend. I don't see any reason she'd lie about it."

It did seem unlikely Stephanie would lie. The question was, why would Tommy? He had to realize that if he'd been in town over the weekend his lie wouldn't hold up in the long run.

The witch had said you had to know what to see. Tommy had shown up at the Zoo claiming to have been in town for just a few hours, during which time he'd heard about Joey and hoped I'd have additional information about the murder. At the time I'd accepted that at face value, but now that I thought about it I realized there had to be more to it.

Chapter 9

"You look adorable," I told Alex later that afternoon. We were upstairs and I was helping her put on her costume in preparation for the Halloween dance at Zimmerman Academy.

"Tony is going to dress as a pirate too. He thought it would be fun if we matched. How's my hair?"

"It's great. Zak is already at the dance, so Tony's mom is going to pick you up. Zak will bring you home, though."

Alex twirled in front of the mirror. "How come you aren't coming if Zak is?"

"I'm going to do something with Scooter. The rain stopped, so we'll probably go to the Hamlet. He was going to spend the night with Tucker, but Tucker got sick."

Alex let out a long breath. "I'm kinda nervous."

"I remember my first school dance," I said. "I was in the seventh grade and I was sure I was going to trip over my own feet when I got out on the dance floor. But

I didn't. I had fun, and I'm sure you will too."

"I hope my hands don't get all sweaty if we dance a slow dance."

I hugged Alex. "Things are going to be fine. Remember, Tony is probably just as nervous as you are."

"You think so? He is in high school and I'm sure he's gone to a lot of dances."

I thought about Alex's friend. He was an extremely intelligent fourteen-year-old who was as socially awkward as he was brilliant. I had a feeling he didn't have a whole lot more experience dancing with the opposite sex than Alex did.

"Maybe he's been to a lot of dances and maybe he hasn't," I answered. "He chose to hang out with you tonight and I'm sure you're going to have a wonderful time. Just relax and remember that all that's really going on is that you're hanging out with a good friend."

"Yeah, you're right. I'm sure it'll be fine."

"It'll be better than fine. Go and have the time of your life and then you can tell me all about it when you get home."

Alex hugged me. "Thanks, Zoe. Wish me luck."

"Luck."

After Alex left I knocked on Scooter's door to ask him what he wanted to do that evening. I could tell he was a little mad he hadn't been allowed to go to the dance with Alex. Zak and I had discussed allowing him to attend, but the dance was for Zimmerman Academy students and their dates, and Scooter didn't attend the Academy. Besides, Scooter really was too immature for a high school dance. Alex was the same age, but she was much, much more mature than her honorary brother.

"Is the maze open?" Scooter asked.

"I'm not sure. It's stopped raining, so maybe. We can drive by to check it out if that's what you want to do."

"Is it going to be haunted again this year?"

"Yes, I believe they planned to add a haunted element at night. In fact, some of the ghosts and ghouls who signed up to do the haunted house are doing the maze instead, so it should be extraspooky this year. Be sure to dress warm. Even though the rain has stopped it's still pretty nippy out there."

Scooter chatted nonstop as we drove through the festively decorated town. While Alex could be quiet and introspective, it seemed at times that

Scooter never shut up. Not that I minded. It made my heart warm to see him so happy and well adjusted. There'd been a time not all that long ago when I'd worried that the lonely little boy would never have the chance of a normal life. There was no doubt about it; Zak and I were rescuers. Whether it was animals or children, if there was a spirit in need we were there to fill the void.

"I hope Tucker is better by Halloween. We were going to hang out and go trick-or-treating."

"I hope so too. If not, I'm sure Alex will go with you. Did Zak help you with your costume?"

"I wanted to be a ninja, but all the ninja costumes were sold out, so Zak was going to try to order one on line. It's not here yet, but he said he paid for express shipping, so we should have it by tomorrow. I hope it's black, like the one in the picture."

"I'm sure if you ordered a black one that's what they'll send you. Do you want to grab some dinner first or go to the maze?"

"Maze. I hope it's really scary, not just something for babies."

"I'm sure it will be very scary."

"Do you think there'll be zombies?"

"Zombies are very popular right now, so I'm going to say that yes, there'll most likely be zombies. Let's not forget a flashlight. The maze has lights, but I remember there were some pretty dark passages last year. I'd hate to get lost."

"Isn't that the point?"

"Yeah, I guess, but I'm pretty hungry, so I'd prefer not to get too lost."

Scooter and I had a wonderful time at the maze. We did get lost, but in a fun way, and by the time we found our way out we were both ready for pizza. It seemed as if half the people in town had the same thought because the place was packed, but we managed to find two stools at the counter.

"Look, there's Levi," Scooter announced after we'd settled in.

I looked where Scooter was pointing. Levi was seated in a booth with Rachael and her daughter, who looked even more like she might be related to him now that they were sitting side by side. All three occupants of the small booth were laughing and smiling, so I assumed the purpose of the gathering hadn't been to inform Levi he was a daddy. As obvious as it seemed to appear to me that Levi could very well have a daughter, I really hoped for Ellie's sake that I was imagining the resemblance.

"Can we go say hi?" Scooter asked.

"We might lose our seats."

"Can I go say hi while you save the seats?"

"Sure. I guess that would be okay."

I watched Scooter as he trotted across the restaurant. He greeted Levi, who must have asked Scooter who he was with because he turned and pointed at me. Levi waved and I waved back. There was a knot in the pit of my stomach as I considered the implications of Levi and Rachael becoming a couple whether they shared a child or not.

It looked as if Rachael was introducing Scooter to her daughter, which I supposed was a good thing because they would be going to the same school as of Monday. Scooter, in his usual fashion, chatted a mile a minute until our pizza arrived and I had to wave him back over. Levi got up and accompanied him when he returned to where we were sitting.

"It looks like we had the same idea. I would have invited you to join us, but we were just finishing up when Scooter came over."

"Are you heading out to the events?"

"Yeah. I thought I'd show Rachael and Joslyn around. Scooter said you went to the maze."

"We did. It was fun. There were a lot of monsters around every turn and they set the hay bales up a little differently this year, so it wasn't the same route as last year."

"We got lost, but it was a fun lost," Scooter contributed.

"I'll definitely have to check it out. If Joslyn doesn't want to go, I'll head over there later."

"Are you planning on spending the night at our place again?"

"No. I only did last night because Ellie looked panicked and I wanted to help relieve her stress. I really don't think I'm in any immediate danger and I want to get an early start in the morning before the game."

Levi turned and motioned to Rachael that he'd be just a minute.

"I'd forgotten that you and Rachael dated senior year until I ran into her the other day," I fished.

"For a while. She dated Tommy before me and Joey after, so I won't go so far as to say what we had was really special, but we had fun. And we're having fun now."

Levi certainly wasn't acting like a man who suspected he might be a father. Either he didn't notice the resemblance or he had no reason to suspect the possibility. Scooter had polished off two slices of pizza while Levi and I had been chatting.

"Someone was hungry," I commented.

"I was, but I'm done now. Can we go back out?"

"You may be finished, but I haven't even started," I reminded the boy.

"Scooter can come with us if he wants and it's okay with you. It'd be nice for Joslyn to have someone her own age along, and if Scooter goes with us you can eat your pizza in peace and quiet. I'll drop him by your house later."

"Can I?" Scooter asked with a huge grin on his face.

Part of me wanted to say no. Part of me wanted this time alone with Scooter. I'd spent a lot of one-on-one time with Alex but much less with Scooter, who tended to hang out with Zak. Still, based on the look of expectation on his face, it was clear what Scooter wanted.

"Yeah, that's fine. I'll see you both at the house later."

As soon as Scooter left with Levi, I ditched my soda and ordered a glass of wine. I watched the television over the bar while I nibbled on my pizza and sipped my wine. The movie of the night happened to be *Funny Farm* with Chevy Chase, which seemed like a perfect fall movie. I laughed along with the dialogue. I'd forgotten how funny the movie could be. When they got to the fake Christmas scene at the end I was reminded that things really weren't always what they seemed to be. I had to wonder which part of my current investigation, if any, was nothing more than an illusion.

"Anything else?" the bartender asked.

"No, just the check."

"Heard you were looking into Joey's murder. Any news?"

"No," I answered. "I'm afraid not. Were you and Joey friends?"

"He came in for pizza a couple times a week. He sat at the bar and we chatted."

I looked around. The restaurant had cleared out quite a bit while I was eating and the bar was almost deserted except for me and a couple at the other end. "If you spoke to Joey recently had he said anything that might explain why someone would want to kill him?"

The bartender took my empty wineglass and set it in the tub under the bar. "Not really. Joey did seem to have demons he was fighting, though. Especially the last month or so. To tell you the truth, he pretty much stopped ordering pizza in favor of whiskey a few weeks before he died."

"Did he ever come in with anyone?"

"There was a guy. Rocco. I guess he used to play football with Joey back in the day. Sometimes they'd meet up here and talk about their glory days. It was kind of sad."

It must be sad if you believed your best days were behind you.

"Did they meet with or talk to anyone else?"

The bartender began wiping down the bar with a white towel. "Not that I can think of. I did hear them talking about someone, however. Seems that one or both of the men were in to some woman named Lisa."

I wasn't sure who Lisa was, but I did know Rocco. He worked at the bowling alley. If I was lucky he would be working and I could get the rest of the story.

Ashton Falls Bowl was a smallish place with just a dozen lanes. It had been in the same place since as far back as I could remember, and by the look of things it had never been updated once. All the lanes were occupied, making for a noisy environment as the colorful balls hit the white pins.

"Hey, Rocco," I greeted the man standing behind the counter.

"Hey, Zoe. I'm afraid we're full up."

"Not a problem. I'm actually here to talk to you, if you have a minute."

"I've got a minute unless someone comes up."

"I guess you heard about Joey?"

Rocco's lips got tight, but he didn't comment.

"I'm helping Salinger look into things and I heard the two of you were friends. I was just wondering if you knew anything at all that might help us."

"I wouldn't say we were close friends. We used to meet up for a beer every now and then. We kept our conversations pretty causal, but I will say he seemed to change after he hooked up with Lisa."

"Lisa?"

"Some dame he met a couple of months ago. He said he was lonely and enjoyed her company, but the woman was a loon. I guess crazy must be contagious because the longer Joey hung out with that broad, the loonier he got."

I crossed my arms on the counter and leaned in just a bit. "What do you mean by crazy?"

"Angry. Paranoid."

"Do you know where I might find her?"

"Haven't seen her since Joey died."

"Do you know her last name?"

Rocco paused. "No. I'm not sure I ever knew it. Joey did mention once or twice that she worked over at the seasonal store, so I guess you could ask around over there if you really want to talk to her."

"Thanks. I'll do that."

When I arrived at the Halloween store it was packed from front to back. Everyone who had put off buying costumes until the last minute seemed to be there tonight. I looked around for someone I knew, hoping they could point out an employee named Lisa. Given the seasonal nature of the store, the staff tended to turn over fairly often, but I'd been in several times recently and knew a friend from high school could be found in the back, mending and repackaging opened and damaged costumes.

"Looks like you have your work cut out for you," I greeted her.

"Tell me about it. I don't know why the customers feel the need to open every package. We provide samples for people to look at, but apparently that isn't good enough. Are you here looking for a costume?"

"Actually, I'm looking for a person. Lisa? I was told she works here."

"She did work here. She quit without notice yesterday. Talk about lousy timing. We're expecting a busy weekend with everything that's going on in town."

"Do you know Lisa's last name, or maybe her phone number or address?"

"I don't have her contact information. You'd have to get that from the personnel office, and everyone in there has gone home for the day. I think her last name was Payne, or maybe Payton. Something like that."

I used to know a Lisa Payton—Tommy's sister—but she'd moved away years ago. "Do you know how old this Lisa is?"

"I guess around eighteen. I know she used to live in the area and just recently moved back. She seemed to like it here, but I guess she must have decided to split. I can't think of any other reason she'd up and quit the way she did."

"Okay, well, thank you for your time. And good luck with the weekend."

I left the store and decided to call Salinger to fill him in on what I'd learned that evening. When I got his cell he suggested I come by the office. I figured I had a while before Levi brought Scooter home and I was just down the street from the county offices, so I headed over there.

"So what's on your mind?" Salinger asked when we'd settled into his office.

"I have new information."

"Shoot."

"First of all, I found out that Joey had been hanging out with someone named Lisa just before his death. Tommy Payton has a sister named Lisa who's a bit younger than he is. Based on my best guess as to the age difference, I'm going to say Lisa is around eighteen now."

"And you think Joey was dating Tommy's little sister?"

"I don't have any hard evidence, but that would be my guess."

Salinger leaned forward so his elbows rested on his desk. "We know Joey and Tommy had been friends for a long time. It seems reasonable that Joey would know Tommy's sister."

"Maybe. I feel like her presence in Joey's life combined with the fact that Tommy and Joey were involved in some sort of an argument might be relevant."

"I guess it wouldn't hurt to track this woman down and have a chat with her. Anything else?"

"I also found out that Joey had been hanging out with a guy named Rocco who works at the bowling alley. I asked him about Joey, but he didn't seem to have any information that could help us track down his killer. Still, it might not hurt for you to speak to him as well."

"Okay, I will. Is that it?"

"No. I also heard through the grapevine that Tommy didn't come into town on Wednesday, as he'd originally told me he did. Stephanie Bird told Ellie that she had drinks with Tommy over the weekend."

Salinger frowned. "It sounds like you're almost building a case for Tommy as the shooter, but let's not forget he was a victim too."

"I know, but this case is so odd, I feel like we need to stay on top of every clue no matter how minor. You never know when some small detail could end up providing just the clue we need to solve this thing."

Salinger reached for a file folder that was part of a stack on his desk. "Speaking of new information, I just found out from the medical examiner that Joey had a brain tumor. It was still small, but the neurologist I spoke to said it was located in such a spot that it could very well have affected his behavior."

"So that could explain the paranoia. I wonder if Joey knew about it."

"I haven't been able to find any evidence that he sought medical treatment for a tumor or related symptoms such as headaches. I'm guessing he didn't know."

"Okay, all of this seems like it might be relevant information. Now we just need to figure out how everything fits together."

When I arrived home Levi's car was in the drive. It seemed all my running around had taken longer than I'd anticipated. I hoped he and Scooter hadn't had to wait too long. I knew Levi had wanted to have an early night to be fresh for the game tomorrow.

"Sorry I'm late," I apologized as I walked into the house. "I got a new lead and stopped to chat with Salinger, and I guess it took longer than I realized."

"No problem. We haven't been here long. Scooter went up to his room. He wanted to call Tucker to tell him about the maze. Can we talk?"

I set my backpack down on the table. "Sure. What's on your mind?"

"Somewhere private. Where we can't be overheard."

I glanced at Levi, who had about the most serious look on his face I'd ever seen. "Let's go into Zak's office. We can close the door. No one will overhear us."

I led Levi down the hall to the large room and closed the door behind us. I indicated that Levi should have a seat on the sofa, but he ignored my invitation and began to pace.

"What's on your mind?"

Levi ran his hand through his hair. He looked nervous. "Rachael and I were chatting tonight while the kids played games at the arcade. She told me she'd become pregnant with Joslyn while she was still in high school."

Uh-oh. Here it came. Levi *was* her father!

"She explained how she made the decision not to tell the father and how she had to hide her pregnancy until after graduation, when she was able to leave town." Levi took a deep breath before he continued, and I was pretty certain I'd forgotten to breathe altogether. "While she was telling me everything she went through during that difficult time in her life something occurred to me." Levi looked up and met my eye. I could see he was working up the courage to go on.

"You realized you're Joslyn's father," I blurted out.

"What? No. I'm not Joslyn's father. Why would you think such a thing?"

"I don't know," I defended myself. "You and she have the same coloring."

"A lot of kids have my coloring, but as far as I know I'm no one's father."

I let out a long breath. Talk about relief. "I'm sorry. I guess I jumped to conclusions."

"Rachael told me that Joey was Joslyn's father."

Okay, now that was a new twist. "Did he know?"

"Yeah, he knew. Rachael and Joslyn ran into Tommy five years ago. When he saw Joslyn he suspected Joey might be her father, so he asked Rachael about it. She confided in him that it was true, which I guess made Tommy pretty mad. The thing is, while Joey and I just messed around with Rachael, Tommy really cared about her. She told me that Tommy went to Joey and told him about Joslyn. Tommy felt Joey should step up and help Rachael out financially, but Joey insisted it was her choice to have the kid, and because he was never given the opportunity to have any input on whether or not she kept the baby in the first place, he felt no responsibility for her."

"Ouch."

"Yeah. Joey could be pretty self-centered."

"That must be the argument Tommy referred to."

"I guess. Anyway, can we get back to the reason for this conversation?"

"Sure. I'm sorry. Go ahead. What did you realize when Rachael was talking to you about her pregnancy?"

"Is Ellie pregnant?"

I supposed I should have seen this coming. I'm not sure why I hadn't. "I think that's something you should discuss with Ellie."

"Maybe, but I'm asking you. Best friend to best friend. Is Ellie pregnant?"

Levi frowned when I didn't answer. "She is, isn't she?"

I wasn't sure what to say. Levi actually looked angry. I wasn't expecting angry.

"Answer me!" he shouted. "Is Ellie pregnant?"

"Yes."

Suddenly all the anger left Levi's body and he looked like he was going to cry. "Brady?"

At first I wasn't sure what Levi was asking, but then I realized he was assuming Brady was the baby's father. I guess that made sense; Ellie and Brady had been dating when Ellie conceived. "No, not Brady."

"Then who?"

I just looked at Levi. I watched his expression as he put all the pieces together. "Oh, God, it's me. Ellie is pregnant with my baby."

I got up and crossed the room. I took Levi's hand in mine.

"Why didn't she tell me?"

"She's going to, but she's scared."

"Scared? Of me? Why on earth would she be scared of me?"

"She knows how you feel about having kids. You've made it very clear that you don't want any. I think she feels bad about what happened and doesn't want to ruin your life. She loves you and she cares a great deal about your happiness."

Levi walked over and sat down on the sofa. He didn't say anything, but I could see he was in shock.

"I think it would be best for you to wait to talk to Ellie about this until you've had a chance to process everything," I said softly.

"Yeah," Levi said, his eyes devoid of light. "That might be a good idea."

Chapter 10

Saturday, October 29

Another sleepless night, but this time it had nothing to do with Joey's death or the identity of the possible killer. Poor Levi. Once the reality of the situation sank in, I could see he was completely overwhelmed. It was a lot to take in, especially for a person who'd never really seen himself as a father. It was too bad he'd had all that dropped into his lap the night before the big game, but at least he had something else to focus on. My dilemma, I realized, was that I had no idea whether I should say anything to Ellie. Part of me felt it wasn't my place to get in the middle of it, while another felt I already was in the middle and should warn her about the situation.

"I can't believe how nervous I am," Ellie commented when I picked her up for the game.

"Nervous?"

"About the game. I hope the boys do well. I know everyone has been working really hard and I'd love for them to win."

"Yeah, me too."

"Where are Zak and the kids?"

"They went on ahead. They wanted seats on the fifty-yard line, so they went to the field hours ago. I didn't want to go that early, so they're saving us seats. Do you want to drop Shep over at our place so he isn't alone all day?"

"That would be great. I'll grab him. You might want to move your purse." Ellie nodded to the bag on the backseat. "Shep likes to eat phones."

"It's not my bag, it's Alex's. Zak had this car last night. She must have left it behind when he brought her home. I'll stick it in the trunk for now."

I put the bag in the trunk while Ellie went in to fetch Shep.

"So, did Alex have fun at the dance?" Ellie asked as she came back to the car with the dog.

"She really did." I smiled. "She was talking a mile a minute when she got home, which is a very un-Alex thing to do. I guess the not-a-date turned into a sort-of-date and she got her first kiss."

"Aww. How sweet."

"I thought Zak was going to have an aneurism when Alex proudly announced that Tony had kissed her good night. I really never pegged him as the overprotective-papa type, but he certainly played the role to a T last night. I can't imagine how he's going to be with our own daughter."

"Your daughter? Is there something you aren't telling me?"

"No, I'm not pregnant. I was referring to a metaphorical future daughter."

We dropped Shep at the house, then headed into town and the high school. It was a beautiful sunny day, perfect for football. The sun had dried most of the rain puddles and it looked as if we were in for about as awesome a day as they came. Too bad I was too stressed out to enjoy it.

"So, how's the murder investigation coming along?" Ellie asked as we drove through town.

I filled her in on everything I'd discovered the previous evening.

"After everything we've learned I can't make up my mind about Tommy," Ellie said. "I mean, he did get shot. The fact that he was a victim of whoever is running around with a gun seems to indicate that he isn't the killer—unless the wound was self-inflicted of course."

"Actually, I had a similar thought, but Salinger said the angle was off for his wound to have been self-inflicted."

"Which may let him off the hook as a murder suspect, but he did lie about when he got into town and he did check himself out of the hospital and then basically disappear. Something smells fishy."

"I agree. It also seems significant to me that it appears Joey was dating Tommy's sister. Tommy and Joey had an argument over the way Joey treated Rachael, which would indicate to me that he wouldn't be thrilled with the idea that his baby sister was dating the scumbag who'd turned his back on the woman he loved during her time of need."

"This whole thing is pretty twisted. Do you remember why Tommy and Rachael broke up in the first place?"

I thought about it. "I'm not sure, but I seem to remember that Rachael broke up with Tommy to date Levi."

"Who then dumped her, causing her to hook up with Joey."

I slowed the car and pulled up to a stoplight. I turned and looked at Ellie. "Levi told me that Tommy really cared about Rachael, and I do remember Levi and Tommy having a falling out after Levi started dating Rachael. I wonder if the fact that Tommy showed up in town at the same time Rachael moved back is related."

"You think Tommy was really in town to see Rachael?"

"I think it makes an interesting theory, although if Tommy's sister has moved back to Ashton Falls that could provide a reason for his visit as well."

"I still don't get why he lied about the timing of his arrival. If he was out with Stephanie it seems like he would realize there would be people in town who'd remember seeing them together."

"Yeah, that is strange. I guess he might not realize I would doubt his statement and look into things further. He might have stopped by to talk to me on Wednesday in order to create an alibi for the time Joey was shot." I pulled forward when the light turned green.

"Why would he need an alibi unless he's the one who shot Joey?"

"Exactly." My phone buzzed just as I pulled into the high school parking lot. It was Zak.

"Hey, Zak. We just got here."

"Have you spoken to Levi this morning?"

"No. Why?"

"He's not here. His assistant coach just pulled me aside and let me know he never showed. They've been calling him, but he isn't picking up."

I felt my heart sink to my toes. I couldn't help but remember the witch's words when she informed me that Tommy wasn't the one who was to follow. Surely it wasn't Levi. Though he had been upset last night. Maybe he'd gone home and drowned his sorrows in a bottle of scotch.

"Has anyone gone by his apartment?"

"No. Everyone kept thinking he'd show up any minute."

"I'm going to head over to his place to check on him. I'll call you when I get there."

"What happened?" Ellie asked. Her face was as white as a sheet. I knew I needed to keep it together and not give in to the panic I was feeling for her sake.

"Levi never showed up at the school. I'm heading over to his apartment. Do you want to come or wait here with Zak?"

"I'm coming."

I started the car and pulled out of the lot and back onto the highway. Levi's apartment was only a couple of minutes away. Hopefully we'd find him sleeping off a bender and not... well, I didn't want to think about that.

"Wait here," I said to Ellie when we pulled up in front of the apartment building.

"I'm coming with you."

"I know you want to, but I'm not sure what we'll find, so I think it's best that you and the baby wait while I check it out."

"You think he's the second victim. The one from the note you got that first night."

"I hope not, but at this point I don't know. I'll only be a minute. If I don't come back in two minutes, call 911."

With that I got out of the car and quickly made my way to Levi's unit.

I knocked, but he didn't answer. I tried the doorknob; it wasn't locked. I gasped when I let myself in. It looked like there'd been a struggle. I held my breath as I made my way to Levi's bedroom. The bed was mussed, as if he'd slept in it, and his phone was on the bedside table, but the room was otherwise empty.

There was no way Levi would just have left without taking his phone. Levi was in a serious relationship with his cell and I never saw the two of them apart.

I picked up Levi's phone and put it in my pocket. Ellie was waiting, so I decided to return to the car before I called Salinger. I felt my heart skip a beat when

I found Tommy sitting in the backseat of my car, chatting with Ellie.

"Tommy. What are you doing here?" I asked as calmly as I could. Ellie looked nervous, but at least she wasn't totally freaking out. "I figured you'd be at the big game."

"Figured the same thing about you."

"Levi forgot his phone, so he asked Ellie and me to come pick it up. We're heading back to the school now."

"You're lying. I happen to know Levi didn't ask you anything."

I looked straight into Tommy's eyes. "Is he dead?"

Ellie gasped.

"Not yet. But he will be if we don't hurry."

"Hurry?" I asked.

"Hand me your cell phones. Levi's too."

I took Ellie's and then handed Tommy all three phones.

"Can't have anyone tracking us," Tommy said as he tossed the phones out the window.

"Tracking us where?" I asked.

"Just drive. I'll tell you where to go."

I knew that going along with Tommy without putting up a fight might not be a good idea, but I was worried about Ellie, and I really wanted to see if he was taking us to Levi, so I followed Tommy's instructions. "Do you want to tell me what's going on?" I asked.

"My sister Lisa has Levi and Rachael tied up in an abandoned cabin out on the old highway and is threatening to shoot them. She has it in her warped little head that they wronged me and need to pay for their sins. I tried to talk her into just leaving town with me, but she's adamant that they should pay for what they did to me the same way I made Joey pay for what he did to Rachael."

"Did you kill Joey?"

"It was an accident."

"We need to call Salinger."

"We aren't going to call Salinger. You and I are going to figure a way out of this situation without bringing the cops into it."

I glanced at Ellie, who was as white as a sheet. "What's your plan exactly?"

"We're going to meet up with Lisa and you're going to help me convince her to come with me peacefully. It won't make things better if she kills Rachael and Levi. You have to help me make her see that."

"Convince her how?"

"I don't know. I guess figuring that out will be your problem if you want to save your friends."

I turned off the highway onto the county road that led out to the cabin. "I want to help Levi and Rachael, so I'll do as you ask, but maybe you should tell me exactly what happened so I can figure out the best way to deal with this situation."

I watched Tommy in the rearview mirror as he settled in for what I assumed was going to be a long explanation. "When I heard Rachael was moving back to Ashton Falls I decided to come for the game as a way to spend time with her. I love her, you know. I always have and I always will. We were meant to be together and we most likely would have if not for Levi."

"Levi stole Rachael from you." I was stating a fact I already knew to be true.

"Yeah. And the worst part was, he didn't even want her. Not really. He used her and then he tossed her aside, which is how she ended up with Joey. Did you know Joey was the father of Rachael's daughter?"

I decided not to admit I knew it. I wasn't sure where this whole thing was going, so I decided to keep what I knew close to my chest.

"He didn't want her of course," Tommy continued. "He could have had this beautiful little girl in his life and he wanted nothing to do with her. I tried to fill in and be a father to Joslyn, but Rachael didn't want me hanging around. She didn't understand how much I loved and needed her."

I glanced at Ellie, who was softly crying but otherwise silent.

"So you came to Ashton Falls and shot him."

"I came to Ashton Falls to see Rachael, but when I got here I found out that Joey was sleeping with my sister. My baby sister. She'd just turned eighteen a few months before. I could see he was using her the way he used Rachael and I flipped. I didn't mean to kill him. I just wanted to talk to him, but things got heated, and the next thing I knew he was dead."

I slowed the car and turned onto the dirt drive Tommy indicated.

"Okay, so I get that you shot Joey in a moment of passion, but who shot you?"

"Lisa."

I didn't see that one coming. "Your sister shot you? Why?"

"It was intentional. Once I realized Joey was dead I figured I'd be a suspect if anyone put everything together, so Lisa and I decided if I got shot as well I would be seen as a victim instead."

Apparently crazy ran in the family, although I had to admit Tommy's plan had worked brilliantly. That was exactly what had happened.

"Lisa has a small handgun and she was careful. Stung a bit, but nothing vital was damaged. Things would have been fine if you hadn't started snooping around. I've heard how you always manage to find the killer, so I guess I sort of freaked out when I heard you were investigating."

I pulled up in front of the house. "Which is why you checked yourself out of the hospital. What I don't understand is why you're still in town."

"I couldn't leave without Lisa, and I'm having a harder time than I thought I would convincing her to let bygones be bygones. Lisa isn't right in the head. Never really has been. She gets these ideas in her head and they take root whether they make sense or not. Lisa saw Levi and Rachael together in town last night, which seemed to ignite her irrational side. She's convinced that if Levi hadn't stolen Rachael from me and Rachael hadn't cheated on me with Levi, she never would have ended up with Joey and I wouldn't have had to kill him. She's convinced it's unfair that Levi and Rachael have each other when she and I have ended up alone."

I glanced at Ellie, who looked shocked but still hadn't spoken.

"Lisa really cared about Joey," I realized.

"She really did. The man had changed. I don't know what happened to him, but he ended up being as crazy as she is. I guess she liked that."

This was officially the most absurd investigation I'd ever been involved in, but I knew I needed to get into crazy Lisa's head if I was going to save everyone involved.

I turned and looked into the backseat. "Okay, so Lisa has Levi and Rachael tied up inside. She doesn't think it's fair that they have each other when the two of you don't have anyone, so she wants to punish them. What exactly does she plan to do?"

"She has a gun. She's going to shoot them."

"Why didn't you just take the gun away from her?" I wondered.

"Honestly, I'm not confident she wouldn't shoot me if I tried to interfere. She's seriously grieving over Joey, and in her mind it's Levi and Rachael's fault he's dead. I needed to buy some time to figure things out if I wanted to save Rachael, so

I told Lisa I needed to go into town to get my video camera so we could record Rachael and Levi's confession."

"Their confession?"

"Lisa wants them to confess to everything she's certain they've done to create the current situation. She liked the idea of recording it, so she agreed to wait to kill them until I came back with the camera. I saw you pull up in front of Levi's building as I drove past and got the idea that maybe you could help me talk Lisa into leaving with me without further violence."

"And why did you think I could help?"

Tommy shrugged. "You're smart and resourceful and I knew you'd be motivated. I really didn't plan this whole thing. I just saw you and made a decision."

"Okay, you and I will go in, but Ellie waits here."

"Sorry. We all go in. I want to stop Lisa, not get her arrested, so I need to make sure no one alerts the cops before we get away. Lisa is unpredictable. If you want your friends to live you'll help me convince Lisa to leave with me."

I paused briefly. I was pretty sure I could take Tommy if push came to shove. He was a lot bigger than me, but I was fast and wily. Of course Tommy had a coat on, so I had no way of knowing if he had a gun, plus I really did want to save Levi and if I attacked Tommy, Lisa might very well shoot both her captives. I glanced at Ellie, trying to convey that everything was going to be fine, before I opened the driver's side door and got out. I took Ellie's hand as we slowly walked toward the front door of the old house.

"Why'd you bring them?" Lisa whined when we walked in. Rachael and Levi were tied up and gagged. Both were sitting on wooden chairs near the far wall of the main living area.

I noticed Ellie's eyes lock with Levi's as Tommy answered.

"They stopped by when I went to get the camera. I must have said something to make them suspicious. When they started acting strange I decided to bring them along."

"I wish you hadn't done that. Now we'll have to kill them too."

"What if we just tie these two up too and skip the killing part?" Tommy suggested.

"Levi and Rachael need to die. If not for their cheating, Joey would still be alive. We were going to get married and now I'm alone again. It just isn't right." Lisa lifted her gun and pointed it at Levi's head.

"No. Please, no" Ellie cried.

"Joey's not dead," I blurted out. Okay, that was a wild shot in the dark, but what did I have to lose?

"What do you mean, he's not dead?" Lisa asked.

"I mean when Levi found him and the paramedics showed up he still had a slight heartbeat. It wasn't strong, and without very special equipment you wouldn't even know it. They took him to a special hospital down in the valley and now it looks like he's going to be fine."

Lisa actually looked like she was mulling over my words. I guess a tiny sliver of hope is all it takes to convince the mind that what it wants to believe is real.

"I know everyone has been saying he's dead, but the sheriff thought Joey's life could still be in danger because we didn't know who shot him, so he decided it was better to let people believe he died that day."

"You aren't lying?"

"No, I'm not. I can take you to him if you want."

Lisa lowered the gun just a bit.

Tommy had an odd expression on his face. I doubted that he, like his gullible sister, believed Joey was alive; he was probably trying to decide whether this was part of the plan to get his sister to leave with him.

"Of course the only way I'm going to take you to see Joey is if you let my friends go," I added.

"They need to die after what they did to Tommy and me."

"Maybe, but Joey and Levi are friends, and Joey and Rachael have a child together. How happy do you think he's going to be if you kill them?"

"I guess he might not be happy about that," Lisa admitted.

"So let the others go and I'll take you to Joey."

Lisa lowered her arm.

"I'll take Lisa to see Joey," Tommy countered. "You can give us directions."

I shrugged. "Fine by me. Do you have anything to write with?"

"We should tie them up in case they are lying," Lisa suggested. "If they are we can come back here and kill them."

"That sounds like a perfect idea," Tommy agreed.

After I drew a set of bogus directions Tommy tied up and gagged Ellie and me and the two of them left. It was going to be up to Tommy to prevent Lisa from returning before we could make our escape. I wasn't too worried that we were tied up in a house well off the beaten path and no one knew where we were because I knew Zak would rescue us. He always did.

We didn't have long to wait. As it turned out, when Zak had realized Alex's cell was still in my car he'd tracked it when I didn't call him back right away. He'd then called Salinger, who'd headed to the location Zak had given him, before heading out to the house himself. Zak had arrived seconds after Salinger, who had been turning into the drive just as Tommy was pulling onto the highway. It looked like the crazy siblings wouldn't get away after all.

"Are you okay?" Zak asked as he removed my gag.

"Yeah. Help Ellie. She looks like she's going to pass out."

Zak untied Ellie and then she untied Levi while Zak worked on Rachael's ropes. Eventually Zak got back around to me.

I glanced at Levi, who held Ellie in his arms while she wept. "Let's wait outside," I suggested to Rachael and Zak.

I wasn't sure how things were going to work out, but it did warm my heart to see Levi so totally focused on Ellie. I noticed him place a hand on her stomach, assuming he was asking about the baby, and saw her nod. He pulled her close once again and I watched from a distance while they both cried.

Chapter 11

Monday, October 31

In spite of everything that had happened, Zak and I managed to pull off another spectacular spooktacular on Halloween night. The house was decorated to resemble a magical Halloween town and the food Ellie had prepared with Tiffany's help was both delicious and theme appropriate. It did my heart good to see my friends and family sharing laughs and having good, old-fashioned Halloween fun without the drama of the past week hanging over them. Tucker was feeling better and attended with Scooter after they'd gathered bags full of candy trick-or-treating, and Alex had invited Tony, which had Zak glaring at them the entire evening.

"You don't need to keep giving Tony the evil eye," I said as we watched the young couple.

"She's only twelve."

"Yes, but she's a bright, mature, levelheaded twelve. And Tony is a good kid. I think we can trust they aren't going to engage in any age-inappropriate activities."

Zak didn't answer, but I could see he still wasn't as relaxed about the whole thing as I was.

"Phyllis and the girls are here, and it looks like they all brought dates as well," I commented as our school principal, Phyllis King, walked in with history teacher Ethan Carlton and the three teenage girls who boarded with her and their dates. "And Alex and Tony are joining them, so you can relax."

"Yeah, I guess you're right. I guess I have been a little manic about this. Tony *is* a good kid and Alex can be trusted. I never realized how hard this parenting thing would be until Alex began to think about boys."

"You're a great surrogate dad."

"Sure, to the boys. I don't stress about Pi and Scooter nearly as much as I do about Alex. Maybe we'd better stick with boys when we have children of our own. Less to worry about."

I laughed. "First of all, I don't think we'll have a choice, and second, there's just as much to worry about with boys."

"I'm going to have to disagree with you on that. When Pi lived with us I never once worried that some girl was going to take advantage of him and break his heart, but it seems once Alex announced she was interested in a member of the opposite sex that's been all I can think about."

"It'll get easier once you get used to the idea."

Zak didn't look convinced, but he let the subject drop.

"It looks like Levi and Ellie worked things out," Zak commented.

I glanced across the room where Levi and Ellie were chatting with Jeremy and Jessica. They looked as relaxed and happy as the newlywed couple they were chatting with.

"Yeah. I haven't had a chance to talk to either of them in depth, but Ellie did say they'd talked and Levi very much wants to be part of the baby's life."

"Are they going to get back together?"

"I don't know. I'm not sure they know yet. Ellie indicated that they were taking things slowly and focusing on the baby for the time being."

"That's probably a good idea. Ellie and Levi have a lot of history, both good and bad, to work through. Has Ellie decided how to handle letting everyone else know about the baby?"

"I think she's going to make an announcement tonight. It'll be hard, but almost everyone she's close to is here in one place, so maybe it'll be easier on her. It looks like my parents are here with Harper. I should go over to say hi."

"I need to ask Brady if he's had a chance to speak to Will."

"They were going to talk on the phone?"

Zak nodded. "I wanted the two of them to have a chance to chat before I brought Will here. I could see Brady was a little intimidated by the idea of Will returning when I approached him on Friday, but after I assured him that his job was secure he seemed excited about exploring the options having Will on the staff would create, so I suggested they chat on the phone to get acquainted prior to his arranging a visit."

Zak and I made our separate ways around the room, stopping to chat with our guests. I hadn't really been keeping track, but it looked as if there were more than a hundred people attending this year's party.

"Good turnout and the food is fantastic," I said, greeting Ellie and Levi.

"It really is a good turnout," Ellie agreed. "I'm getting nervous about making my announcement. Do you think I should wait?"

"No, I think you've waited long enough. If you're happy everyone will be happy for you."

Levi laced his fingers through Ellie's. "We'll do it together."

Ellie took a deep breath. "Should we do it now?"

"Now seems as good a time as any."

Ellie nodded.

"Can I have your attention?" I said as loudly as I could to be heard over the noise in the room. Zak hurried over and turned off the stereo, which helped quite a bit. "I want to welcome you all and thank you for coming. I think this might be the best Halloween spooktacular of all."

Everyone clapped.

"The pool is open if anyone is interested, and there's plenty of food and beverages, both of the adult and kid variety. We'll begin the costume contest shortly, but first Ellie and Levi have an announcement to make."

The room became eerily quiet as I turned and looked at Ellie. The poor thing was white as a sheet. Levi put his arm around her shoulders and pulled her close.

He smiled at the crowd and announced: "We're having a baby."

Now the room was completely silent. I could see the look of surprise on the faces of most if not all the partygoers. I was about to say something to break the tension when my grandpa stepped forward and congratulated the expectant parents with warm hugs. Once he broke the ice everyone else followed suit, and before long there was a line of well-wishers waiting to congratulate the expectant parents.

"I can't tell you how relieved I am not to have to keep Ellie's secret anymore," I whispered to Zak.

"Secrets can weigh you down, that's for sure."

I glanced back at Ellie and Levi. They really did look happy. They had a long road ahead of them, but my instinct was that they'd work things out and create a warm, loving home in which their baby could grow and prosper.

My favorite part of any day, no matter how it starts out or the path it takes, is the final moments when Zak wraps me in his strong arms and pulls me close to his body. There's something comforting about being enveloped in a nurturing cocoon as his breath caresses my cheek while we drift together into a world where dreams become reality. On this particular night, however, I found my mind grasping at thoughts that refused to let go.

"Zak," I said softly as I felt his body begin to relax into slumber.

"Hmm?"

"Are you worried that we aren't pregnant yet?"

Zak stiffened somewhat as he struggled toward wakefulness. He turned slightly so that he was looking at me in the dark. "No, I'm not worried. We've only been trying a couple of months. Are you worried?"

"No. Not really. I guess I've just been worried that I'm not more worried."

Zak leaned up on one elbow and looked me in the eye. Although it was dark, the moon outside the window provided enough light for me to see the outline of his face. He ran his finger along my cheek, tucking my hair behind my ear in the process.

"I know that doesn't make any sense. I just wanted you to know how I felt," I added.

"Actually..." Zak rolled onto his back and pulled me to him so that my head was resting on his chest. He wrapped his arms tightly around me and kissed the top of my head. "It does make sense. Having a baby is a big step, and while we both want children very much, we've only been married for a year and things have been pretty crazy lately. I think it's perfectly normal for you to be having doubts."

"Are you having doubts?"

"Sometimes," Zak admitted. "Don't get me wrong; I want to have a baby with you more than anything, but I want us both to be ready."

I used my forefinger to draw figure eights on his chest as we talked. "How will we know when we're ready? And what if we never are?"

I listened to his heartbeat against my ear as he paused before answering. "I wish I had answers for you; for us. I guess we just need to take things as they come. If you told me at this very moment we were expecting I'd be the happiest man in the world, but the fact that we haven't conceived yet doesn't make me sad or concerned. I trust nature to know when the timing is right, and in the meantime I say we just live our lives. We have Scooter and Alex to raise and we have a school to build and friends to support. We have very full lives."

"So you think that when the time is right it'll just happen?"

"I do. For now, maybe we shouldn't look at ourselves as *trying*. I think it's creating unnecessary pressure. Let's just focus on building a life together and let the baby make an appearance when he or she is ready."

I pulled myself on top of Zak and used my free hand to brush the hair from his forehead. "I love you so much and I would never want to do anything to let you down, but I guess I have been worried about all that stuff even though I've tried not to be."

Zak put his hands on either side of my face and looked me in the eye. "I love you; all of you; every molecule, every thought, every fear, every insecurity. You could never let me down."

Zak pulled my face down so our lips met, chasing thoughts of babies, doubts, and uncertainties from my mind.

Recipes

Recipes by Kathi Daley
Pumpkin Muffins
Pumpkin Snickerdoodles
Chicken Casserole
Mexican Lasagna

Recipes by Readers
Aunt Pearlie's Fresh Apple Cake—
submitted by Jeanie Daniel
Pumpkin Rolls—submitted by Nancy Farris
Pumpkin Custard Crunch—submitted by
Robin Coxon
Aunt Lena's Apple Crunch—submitted by
Connie Correll

Pumpkin Muffins

3 cups sugar
1 cup vegetable oil
4 eggs
1 16-oz. can pumpkin (2 cups)
½ cup water
3½ cups flour
2 tsp. baking soda
1 tsp. baking powder
½ tsp. salt
1 tbs. cinnamon
1 tsp. ginger
1 tsp. ground nutmeg
½ tsp. ground cloves
½ tsp. allspice
4 cups walnuts, chopped

Combine sugar, oil, and eggs. Add pumpkin and water and mix well.

Combine dry ingredients and add to pumpkin mixture. Add nuts.

Spoon into greased cupcake pans (or use papers). Bake at 350 degrees for 28–30 minutes.

Cream Cheese Frosting (optional):

¾ cup butter, softened
6 oz. cream cheese, softened
1 tsp. vanilla
3 cups powdered sugar

Whip all ingredients together and spread onto cooled muffins.

Pumpkin Snickerdoodles

1 cup butter (at room temperature)
1 cup granulated sugar
½ cup light brown sugar
¾ cup canned pumpkin
1 large egg
2 tsp. vanilla extract
3¾ cups flour
1½ tsp. baking powder
½ tsp. salt
½ tsp. ground cinnamon
¼ tsp. ground nutmeg

For the coating:

½ cup sugar
1 tsp. cinnamon
½ tsp. ground ginger
Dash of allspice

Whip together butter and sugars until creamy. Add pumpkin, egg, and vanilla. Mix well. Add dry ingredients and mix well.

Refrigerate for at least 1 hour.

In a separate bowl, mix the sugar and spices for the coating. Roll chilled dough into 1-inch balls. Roll in coating.

Bake on ungreased cookie sheet at 400 degrees until lightly brown (around 12 minutes).

Chicken Casserole

1 box (16-oz.) penne pasta
4 chicken breasts, cooked and cubed
1 can Campbell's cream of cheddar soup
1 can Campbell's nacho cheese soup
    (you can use two cans of either if you
like your casserole more or less spicy)

2 cups shredded cheddar cheese
1 cup grated Parmesan cheese
1 jar (16-oz.) Alfredo sauce (any brand)
¾ cup milk
1 cup cashews (or more if you like)
Salt and pepper to taste
Cheddar cheese crackers

Boil pasta according to directions on box
(10–12 minutes).

Meanwhile, mix cooked and cubed
chicken, soups, cheeses, Alfredo sauce,
milk, cashews, and salt and pepper
together in a large bowl.

Drain pasta when tender and add to chicken mixture. Stir until well mixed.

Pour into a greased 9 x 13 baking pan. Top with crumbled cheddar cheese crackers.

Bake at 350 degrees for 30 minutes.

Mexican Lasagna

Preheat oven to 350 degrees. Spray 9 x 13 baking dish with nonstick spray.

Mix in a bowl:

4 large chicken breasts, cooked and cubed
1 cup sour cream
1 cup ricotta cheese
8 oz. diced green chiles (Ortega)
1 package lasagna noodles prepared as directed on box

Sauce:

In a medium saucepan combine:

1 stick butter, melted over medium heat
4 oz. cream cheese, added to melted butter and stirred until smooth
1 cup heavy whipping cream, stirred until blended
1½ cups grated Parmesan, stirred in slowly to avoid lumps

Mix sauce and chicken mixture together.

Grated cheese mixture:

2 cups grated pepper jack cheese
2 cups grated cheddar cheese

Layer ⅓ noodles onto bottom of baking dish.

Place ½ chicken mixture on top of noodles.

Layer ⅓ cheese on top of chicken mixture.

Repeat

Layer final third of noodles.

Top with final third of grated cheeses.

Bake uncovered at 350 degrees for 20–25 minutes. Broil for a few minutes to brown.

Aunt Pearlie's Fresh Apple Cake

Submitted by Jeanie Daniel

1½ cups Crisco oil
2 cups sugar
2 eggs
2 cups flour
1 tsp. baking soda
1 tsp. cinnamon
2 tsp. vanilla
3 cups apples, peeled, chopped, or shredded
1 cup flaked coconut
1 cups nuts (any kind you like; I use pecans)
1 cup raisins

Mix together oil, sugar, and eggs. Sift together flour, baking soda, and cinnamon and stir into the oil mixture. Add the remaining ingredients and pour into greased, floured 9 x 13–inch pan and bake at 350 degrees for 35 to 40 minutes.

Glaze:

½ stick butter
⅛ cup milk
½ cup plus 1 tbs. powdered sugar

Stir together and bring to a boil in a small saucepan and pour over cake while hot.

Pumpkin Rolls

Submitted by Nancy Farris

This is a staple at our office food days. It's good any way: warm, cold, or room temperature. There are never any leftovers!

1 8-oz. pkg. refrigerated crescent rolls
1 8-oz. pkg. cream cheese, softened
1 cup pumpkin
½ cup sugar
1 tsp. vanilla
1 tsp. pumpkin pie spice

¼ cup butter
¼ cup cinnamon sugar (¼ cup sugar mixed with 1 tsp. cinnamon)

Unroll crescent rolls and put half in the bottom of an 8 x 8-inch pan. Flatten and press any seams together.
Mix together cream cheese, pumpkin, ½ sugar, vanilla, and pumpkin pie spice by hand or with hand mixer. Spread over the crescent roll. Place the remaining half of

the crescent roll on top of the cream cheese mixture.
Melt the butter and pour over the top.
Sprinkle with the cinnamon sugar mixture.
Bake at 350 degrees for 30 minutes.

Pumpkin Custard Crunch

Submitted by Robin Coxon

I hope you find these as enjoyable as my family does.

29-oz. can pumpkin
3 eggs, beaten
2 tsp. pumpkin pie spice
1 tsp. cinnamon
14-oz. can sweetened condensed milk
1 cup milk
2 tsp. vanilla extract

Crunch Topping:

Stir together oats, brown sugar, flour, cinnamon, and pecans. Add melted butter, toss to mix. Set aside.

3 cups quick cooking oats, uncooked
1 cup brown sugar, packed
1 cup all-purpose flour
1 tsp. cinnamon
1 cup pecans, crushed

1 cup butter, melted

Mix pumpkin, eggs, and spices well; stir in milks and vanilla. Pour into a greased 9 x 13-inch baking pan. Spoon crunch topping over pumpkin mixture. Bake at 350 degrees for 45–60 minutes, until knife tip comes out clean. Watch carefully so topping doesn't burn. Serve warm.

Tasty topped with whipped topping or a scoop of vanilla ice cream.

Aunt Lena's Apple Crunch

Submitted by Connie Correll

Peel, core, and slice about 5 good-sized apples into a large bowl; add ¾ cup sugar, 1 tsp. cinnamon, toss together until the apples are well coated. Place in a 9 x 9 baking dish and dot with 1 tbs. real butter.

Crunchy topping:

Mix together with a fork until these ingredients make a crumble mixture: ½ cup flour, ½ cup sugar, 1 tsp. baking powder, 2 tbs. real butter, and 1 egg.

Spoon the topping on the apple mixture, bake at 350 degrees for 30–35 minutes.

Note: While most old farmhouses had McIntosh apple trees in their yards, I prefer to use a combination of Gala or Braeburn with Cortland. The macs tend to bake up pretty soft, where the Gala/Braeburn will cook tender but not mush.

This recipe will work well with peaches. You may even try it with other fruits. A little experimenting with the dry ingredients may be necessary. You will need to put the baking dish on a cookie sheet or such as peaches and berries will cook over the edge of the dish.

Books by Kathi Daley

Come for the murder,
stay for the romance.

Zoe Donovan Cozy Mystery:

Halloween Hijinks
The Trouble With Turkeys
Christmas Crazy
Cupid's Curse
Big Bunny Bump-off
Beach Blanket Barbie
Maui Madness
Derby Divas
Haunted Hamlet
Turkeys, Tuxes, and Tabbies
Christmas Cozy
Alaskan Alliance
Matrimony Meltdown
Soul Surrender
Heavenly Honeymoon
Hopscotch Homicide
Ghostly Graveyard
Santa Sleuth
Shamrock Shenanigans
Kitten Kaboodle
Costume Catastrophe
Candy Cane Caper – October 2016

Whales and Tails Cozy Mystery:
Romeow and Juliet
The Mad Catter
Grimm's Furry Tail
Much Ado About Felines
Legend of Tabby Hollow
Cat of Christmas Past
A Tale of Two Tabbies
The Great Catsby
Count Catula – *September 2016*
Cat of Christmas Present – *November 2016*

Seacliff High Mystery:
The Secret
The Curse
The Relic
The Conspiracy
The Grudge

Sand and Sea Hawaiian Mystery:
Murder at Dolphin Bay
Murder at Sunrise Beach
Murder at the Witching Hour – *September 2016*

Zimmerman Academy:
The New Normal

Ashton Falls Cozy Cookbook

Road to Christmas Romance:
Road to Christmas Past

From Henery Press:
Pumpkins in Paradise
Snowmen in Paradise
Bikinis in Paradise
Christmas in Paradise
Puppies in Paradise
Halloween in Paradise
Treasure in Paradise – April 2017

Kathi Daley lives with her husband, kids, grandkids, and Bernese mountain dogs in beautiful Lake Tahoe. When she isn't writing, she likes to read (preferably at the beach or by the fire), cook (preferably something with chocolate or cheese), and garden (planting and planning, not weeding). She also enjoys spending time on the water when she's not hiking, biking, or snowshoeing the miles of desolate trails surrounding her home.

Kathi uses the mountain setting in which she lives, along with the animals (wild and domestic) that share her home, as inspiration for her cozy mysteries.

Kathi is a top 100 mystery writer for Amazon and she won the 2014 award for both Best Cozy Mystery Author and Best Cozy Mystery Series.

She currently writes four series: Zoe Donovan Cozy Mysteries, Whales and Tails Island Mysteries, Sand and Sea Hawaiian Mysteries, and Seacliff High Teen Mysteries.

Giveaway: I do a giveaway for books, swag, and gift cards every week in my newsletter, The Daley Weekly **http://eepurl.com/NRPDf**

Other links to check out:
Kathi Daley Blog – publishes each Friday
http://kathidaleyblog.com

Webpage – **www.kathidaley.com**

Facebook at Kathi Daley Books –
www.facebook.com/kathidaleybooks

Kathi Daley Teen –
www.facebook.com/kathidaleyteen

Kathi Daley Books Group Page –
https://www.facebook.com/groups/569578823146850/

E-mail – **kathidaley@kathidaley.com**

Goodreads –
https://www.goodreads.com/author/show/7278377.Kathi_Daley

Twitter at Kathi Daley@kathidaley –
https://twitter.com/kathidaley

Amazon Author Page –
https://www.amazon.com/author/kathidaley

BookBub –
https://www.bookbub.com/authors/kathi-daley

Pinterest – **http://www.pinterest.com/kathidaley/**